Tale of Two Ends

Betrayal ~ Divorce ~ Recovery

by

Edward M. Krauss

ISBN: 978-0-9742161-6-4
Library of Congress Control Number: 2023952419

Published by Global Authors Publications

"Filling the GAP in Publishing"

Editing by Kathy Barnett
Cover Art by Kathy Barnett

Printed in the U.S.A. for Global Authors Publications

Dedication

For Esther

"Things are never quite as scary
when you've got a best friend."

Bill Watterson
Calvin and Hobbes

The author thanks and acknowledges the staff and resources of the nationally acclaimed Columbus Metropolitan Library, without which assistance this novel would have been difficult to complete.

Chapter One

Near Boston, Massachusetts about 1980.....

Carole had been at the convention two days, then in the motel for two, and she knew she had to talk to Ernestine soon. It was Saturday morning, and Carole checked out of the motel and went back to the house. She chose to think of it as the house, not home, would not let the word home into her head. "I am going to the house. Tonight I will stay in the house. If we really get divorced maybe I'll sell the house."

She pulled into the driveway, noticing the lawn needed mowing, something Ken often did Saturday mornings. There was an unwritten rule, well heeded in the neighborhood, that Saturday mowing did not start until after 8:00, Sundays a little later. There was a medium-sized stack of mail just inside the front door mail chute, some to Ken, which he apparently had decided to get later. Maybe an excuse to come back to the house to talk to her, confront her. Walking through the rooms Carole felt disconnected, like she was visiting a familiar location, but not one with which she had an emotional connection. She walked into the bedroom, noting that his side of the walk-in closet was completely bare. The bathroom had nothing of a man in it; no shaving implements except her ladies electric, no deodorants except hers, no aftershaves, only perfumes. She walked back in the bedroom, wondering if she could sleep in that bed, wondering what a new mattress cost, but not coming to any decision. She went into the kitchen, sat on a stool at the counter and called her sister, a ritual practiced many times.

"Hello?"

"Hey, hello yourself."

"Well I was about to call you! How was the convention? Eat any lobster on the expense account?"

The words rushed out in one breath. "I came home early and found Ken having sex with Sukie Powers and he is gone, cleaned out his closet."

There was silence at the other end, not a sound. "Ernie?" Permission was given only to her sister and husband to use that name, preferably in private.

"Oh Carole, oh Carole." Ernestine was crying, many tears down her face, her nose almost instantly running. "Oh Carole, what are you doing, what...do you want to come here? Oh, oh I am so sorry, so sorry, please come, I want to hug you. Wait a minute, I have to blow my nose."

Carole heard the sounds of the tissue being pulled from the box and the rather loud nose blowing. When Ernestine came back on the phone Carole said "I can't, not now. I have lots of work to do."

"Are you kidding? To hell with that."

"No, it really is important to me, big projects, and I care about the place, you know that, I can't just not show up Monday. So, how are the kids?"

"The kids are fine and would love to see you. They are always asking for Jamie and Aunt Carole and Uncle --. Oh shit. Sorry."

"It's OK, just no Uncle Ken for a while. Make that maybe never."

"How are you?"

"Well, I am alive, I have an appetite, my digestion works ---"

"Thank you for that information" Ernestine injected. Carole continued "--I go to work, I do my work, I sleep -- well, I guess I should tell you, I haven't been home since -- stayed at a motel, miserable mattress. My back is killing me. Wait a minute."

Carole set down the phone, opened the refrigerator, and got out a bottle of milk. It was about three-quarters full. She sniffed the contents and was pleased that it was not sour, then she opened the cherry-stained cupboard, took out a large glass decorated with delicate blue flowers on thin white stems, and filled it. After putting the bottle away, she bent down as she passed the phone and shouted "Be right there! Milk and cookies time!" She started to take a few from the bag of chocolate chips, and then just grabbed the bag and brought it and the milk to the phone.

"I'm back. Chocolate equals love."

"Oh Carole, I don't know what to say. I just don't. How are you? Never mind, we did that."

"Why don't you ask me what Ken said?"

"You don't have to tell me."

"Why not? He -- he wants out. Deeevorce. Wants a divorce."

"Sukie. I remember her a little, unusual name. Where did I meet her?"

"We met at the book club, you know, a bunch of us read the same book and talk about it every few months. You came as my guest once."

"Yeah, that's it. Sukie, hmm?"

"I liked her. Interesting. I guess Ken liked her too."

Ernestine rubbed her eyes with her free hand. "So what happens now?"

"Well, I, we talked, briefly, no apology, and he sounded so weird, just says he wants out. I want us to go to a counselor, at least try to save it. I just can't see myself saying 'oh, OK, yeah now it's over.' I've got to see if it can be saved, if it is worth it, this makes not much sense, does it?"

"What are you going to say to Jamie? She comes home,

when, next Saturday?"

"Yes. I haven't been thinking a whole lot on that. First, I don't know if we really are through. I just don't know. So depending on where we are when she comes home, guess I'll tell her that Daddy and I had a terrible argument and that he moved out but we're trying to fix things. I don't know. A lot is up to him. I mean, if he wants to sit her down and say I am divorcing your mother -- well, ask me again after I've talked to her, and he has, and -- I don't know. Just don't know. Saying those words a lot, aren't I?"

"You're prepared to forgive him." A statement.

The sisters who love each other so much, tightly bonded since infancy, sat and listened to each other breathe for a moment. Carole sat on her stool, leaning on the counter, cookie crumbs and an almost empty glass of milk in front of her. Ernestine sat on the floor in the family room (disaster room, Larry calls it) just off the kitchen, phone with the long extension cord next to her. They each clearly pictured the other. Behind her Max played with his trucks, Ernestine careful to turn her body so that he did not see her tears. Larry and the girls were gone, shopping for new shoes.

Carole started to cry, softly, as did her sister. "Ernie, I know I should be mad, and I am, I'm mad and insulted and very humiliated. I imagine the whole neighborhood knows by now. But I love him. I love him, the miserable shit. I just do. I mean, if a man says 'I don't want to do this anymore, I'm leaving, I'm'-- oh, what was the phrase in that song?"

"Late for the door"

"That one -- so one says he is late for the door and the other person just says 'cool, see ya', no effort to save or fix it?"

Ernestine blew her nose again, then said "Honey, I'm not going to tell you what to say, what to do, but can I ask you this? What happens the next time you go out of town? Can you ever trust him again?"

Carole did not answer immediately; she had gotten off the stool and taken off her shoes and was standing with her knees stiff and bending way forward and backward, stretching that tight place in the small of her back. "Can I trust him again? Don't you wonder how many times one woman has said that to another? Can I trust him, can you trust him, can we trust him -- again. Ever again."

"Millions of times?"

"And that is just in English!"

They both laughed, then Carole told Ernestine that she wanted to do some chores and maybe take a nap.

"Wait, Carole, when am I going to see you? I need to hug on you."

"Tell you what. I'll take Friday off. I'll pack Thursday morning and leave work by noon, then I can drive to the camp Saturday, get Jamie and tell her. Tell her on the way back, what a great way to end a vacation. I'm not sure what to say. We'll talk, I'll rehearse something."

"Drive safely, see you for dinner Thursday. Meat loaf, mashed potatoes, green beans or peas -- your choice, ice tea, red Jell-O with fruit cocktail, chocolate chip cookies."

"Comfort food."

"Indeed." They hung up, promising to speak again soon.

That night, after the children were asleep, Ernestine told Larry that she had to talk to him about something important. As was their habit, they headed for the kitchen. Larry had found an old metal kitchen table at an antique store, rusty with flaking paint but not too dinged up, and he had cleaned it and worked a few of the dents out, repainted it in their garage. It had a hard white enamel paint top, impervious to spilled grape jelly, the only thing to have with smooth peanut butter. Actually, Larry preferred crunchy, but if he did not make sure there was also smooth in the house he faced the wrath of the little ones. He finished it off with a red trim around the side, as he remembered the table in his grandmother's kitchen. They sat at the table as they always did for serious talks; the bed was for reading and sleeping and making love, not for serious talks. He made jasmine tea, a mutual favorite, careful to remove the teabag before it was bitter. Larry poured tea for both of them and waited.

"Larry" she started, and almost instantly the tears came, not a flood but a slow trickle down the cheeks.

He was instantly upset. "Please, dear heart, what?"

"OK, OK, Ken screwed this girl, this divorced woman I think, neighbor, screwed her in their house and Carole caught him and he wants a divorce."

Larry turned his head, shut his eyes as if the words were a blow to the face, then looked at her. "He wants the divorce -- do you mean she?"

"No -- he, because she wants to try to save it, maybe. Carole's not sure, but I guess he told her -- he is sure."

"How is Carole?"

"You know my big sister can be strong. She is doing that strong thing right now. Talking about how she has work to do and can't take time off until next weekend, how she wants to get them into counseling and maybe save it."

"She's coming next week?"

"Yes, Thursday by dinner, stay through Saturday morning and go pick up Jamie from camp."

"Does Jamie know?"

"No, Carole wants to talk about that, do some rehearsing for…rehearse what to tell Jamie on the ride home."

"I'll baby-sit Friday afternoon if you two want to get away, go to the mall and crush some plastic, have lunch--."

"You are very sweet and the best of husbands. Thank you, we may just do that."

He leaned back, holding his mug of tea balanced on the small roundness that was developing above his belt, the tummy of a contented man. He narrowed his eyes slightly and gave her a half smile. "Am I getting a bit of a look?"

"What look, what?"

"The 'everything is fine between us I don't have to worry about you fucking the neighbors, do I? look', that one."

"I fear not. You are my trusted companion, my one true

love, and you are getting no such look. Of course, if you ever prove me wrong, I will use toenail clippers to remove your penis one clip at a time."

Larry looked at his wife with wide eyes and mock horror. "I didn't know you were capable of such thoughts. Never say penis-destruction things to a man, even in the lightest jest. Now I will have to carry that picture in my head forever."

"Exactly my wish. You think of that should any neighbor lady ask if you can come out and play."

They had not talked or planned or flirted about sex that night, but thinking about this disaster so close to home haunted them both while doing end-of-day chores and brushing their teeth. In bed, as with one mind, they pulled at each other and had hot intense sex, coming almost at the same moment and clinging to each other afterward, he soon falling asleep, she awake a while longer staring into the dark.

Chapter Two

A few days earlier......

The two naked wet people stood and stared at the one naked dry person, no one covering up, just staring. Carole had come home from the convention almost twenty-four hours early, heard the shower going, took off her clothes and walked in to see Ken and her neighbor Sukie washing each other. She ran back to her clothes, dressed as she stumbled down the hallway, grabbed her keys and purse, briefcase and overnight case where she had left them in the living room. Carole threw the things in the car and drove, just drove, then pulled into the well-lit, large parking lot of a cafeteria-style restaurant and sat there. She shook her head, shook it like water in her ears, blinked, sat there. A middle-aged couple pulled into the lot, their car facing hers, and they stared at her as they got out. Carole knew she must have seemed a little nuts, sitting in a car mumbling and shaking her head. "Oh, well" she said, as though someone had dropped an unloved teacup. Don't care about the teacup, just got to clean it up. Not sure what she would say when she got back home, she was surprised and relieved to find no one there when she returned, although gone less than an hour.

Carole walked through the house, not touching things. She had heard the cliché about feeling violated – violated! –

after a burglary, about the home feeling unclean, and that is how it felt to her. She walked into the bedroom and stared at the unmade bed. They had been right there, right there, fucking in that bed. My bed. Our bed. Carole suddenly had to vomit, and just made it to the toilet in time. She cleaned up, changed clothes, packed some clothes and cosmetics. It wasn't until she was blocks away that she realized she hadn't locked the door. Another "Oh, well."

Jamie was at summer camp in New Jersey and would be until the following weekend. Time later to figure out what to say, plan how to say it when their daughter is soon to come home. Not right now. Carole ran through a short list of places she could go, friends, but she sure didn't want to tell them, didn't want the telling of the story, the sitting there while they said how sorry. Without really thinking about it Carole drove away from her neighborhood, away from the familiar streets and stores and buildings, to a strip of small motels and trailer parks and discount drug stores. She chose a motel at random, got a room and found it to be cleaner than she expected with an over-used mattress but good water pressure in the shower. OK for a while. She went to bed, stunned and scared and angry, but so exhausted she was soon asleep.

Although she was not due in the office for another day, there seemed nowhere else to go, nothing better to do. Go to work, return to the familiar, and so she did, feeling disconnected, unreal. Begin to sort things out after five o'clock.

Near the end of the business day the phone rang. "Carole Tagee."

"Have you retained an attorney yet?"

The first words. "Retained." Had he ever used that word with her before? Retained water, retained memories, retained love....none of those. "Have you retained an attorney yet?" Charming.

Carole paused, took a very deep breath, and said "Attorney?" all the while her head was buzzing, a real buzzing sensation like a fly inside her skull, her hands cold. She took another deep breath, staying so calm.

"Yes, Carole, people need attorneys to get divorced." He delivered the line with calm patience and a thin veneer of arrogance, and she was livid. She wanted to slap him, hard.

Speaking with soft intensity so he would hear her heat but the co-workers would not, she said, as fast as she could speak, "How are you, Carole? I'm sorry I cheated on you, Carole. I'm sorry I humiliated you and broke your heart, Carole. Forgive me, Carole."

Silence.

And the silence continued. "So," she said, as airily as she could muster, "I don't want to talk to you right now," and hung up immediately. Her skin burned, the fly vibrated her whole body.

Pete, from accounting, walked into her cubicle seconds after she hung up and started speaking to her profile. "We got approval to move ahead on the Sanford loans, so I wonder if..." Carole turned toward him, determined to keep control. "You OK? You look kinda flushed, getting a fever?"

"No, just--got some personal problems, bad phone call."

"I sure can come back, Sanford's been waiting for a month for approval, another day won't kill 'im."

"No, really, sit down, I'd rather do business than think about--. So it has been approved? Good, they must be tired of waiting. How much over prime?"

Her cubicle at work was private enough for most conversations, but she wanted none of the important words she had to say to be heard by others, so she had told them she would be a little late to work the next day. She got up from the lumpy bed, ate a muffin she had purchased the night before, got completely ready, but instead of going to work she sat on the edge of the bed, moved to the one chair, back to the bed, watched the digital clock tick 8:27, 8:28, 8:29. She dialed Ken's number at work at 8:30.

"Ken Tagee, may I help you?"

"Ken, I'm not getting a lawyer, not doing anything until we sit down and talk. We have been married for thirteen years and suddenly we only talk through attorneys? I want us to go to a marriage counselor. I love you."

She hadn't planned on saying she loved him, the words a surprise, and as soon as she said them she choked up, just could not talk. Sitting on the edge of the bed, dressed for work, she bent over and put the phone against her thigh while she covered her mouth with the other hand. Several seconds went by, she raised her head and the phone to her ear.

"Carole?"

"I'm here."

"Carole, I don't want to go to a counselor. You want to talk, let's meet someplace, but I want to end this, there is nothing to fix." Brief pause. "Don't love me."

Determined not to lose it again, she went quickly on. "Have you been home?"

"No."

She didn't ask. "Well, I haven't either, and I think the front door is unlocked. Could you stop by when you have a moment and check?"

"Carole, move back into the house. Jamie will be coming home, I'm sure this will be very upsetting to her. We have to talk about that -- but right now just move back, will you please? I'll have all my things out of there by--. I can't leave early today, but I'll have all my things out of there by five tomorrow. Please, I'll clean out, and then we can talk. I have to leave for a meeting in about an hour, so after its over I'll swing by and check everything and grab some shirts and things and lock the door. Tomorrow you can come home."

"Home."

"I don't want to be ugly or mean or say anything mean. I don't want to go to a counselor. I want--please get an attorney and let's get this over with."

She paused before saying anything so she could be in complete control. "I want to know something."

"What?"

"If I hadn't caught you were you going to ask for a divorce anyway or keep on cheating?"

He inhaled and blew out his breath, weary confession sound. "I was going to tell you soon, I just hadn't decided when or how. But soon."

"And have sex with me before you told me?"

"Sure, why not?"

They both sat there, holding their phones, she stunned and wondering what to say next, he somewhat startled by the coldness of his answer.

She spoke first, coldly. "My goodness, what a fine, gentlemanly thing to say."

"Carole, look, I'm sorry. That was shitty. I'm sorry; you didn't deserve that. You don't deserve any of this. I want a divorce; I'm not mad at you. You're a good person; please don't make me do the counseling thing. Work with me on this and we can cut a good deal."

"Cut a good deal? Have you lost your mind? Who are you? Where is my husband?" She felt the choking return and banged down the phone.

Chapter Three

Back to work Monday was the start of a lonely, strange week -- Jamie at camp and Ken at -- Sukie's? As it passed Carole became more and more anxious to see her dear sister, and sweet Larry and the three children. The first night back in the house she had gone to sleep on the couch, but it was a poor sleep and her neck started hurting, so at one-forty-five she went into the bedroom and quickly stripped the bed; quick jerky movements with her head held back and up as if the sheets and pillowcases were foul, as if to save her nose from the sharp odor of betrayal. She wadded them up, paused a minute, and went to and out the back door, lifted the lid on the metal garbage can, threw the offending fabrics in and started to lower the lid hard, but set it down gently; nothing to be gained by scaring the neighbors. She told herself that if there were any new stains on the mattress pad, or if it smelled of strange perfume, she would throw it away, maybe the whole mattress, maybe the whole bed. But there were no signs or smells, nothing to speak of the deed, the infidelity. Carole considered washing and drying the mattress pad but she was too tired, so she made up the bed, one pillow only, and went to sleep. The next night she went to bed without a second thought - it was her bed.

Carole could be strong, could be focused. That is what she did the whole week. So as not to call attention to herself she worked hard and concentrated on her tasks and stayed a little late in the office, ate normal food and acted like a normal person. She did notice that it was easier to get going in the morning, in fact she found she could sleep twenty minutes longer and still have plenty of time. No Ken, no married couple's bathroom maneuvers. She realized that sharing a bathroom with him had cost her twenty minutes a morning. Sharing a bed with him cost her a broken heart. Not a good idea to think of Ken while alone in the house. Was he staying with Sukie? Not a good idea to wonder.

When she called Ernestine to confirm the plans, Carole and her sister agreed not to let the children have any inkling that anything was wrong, simply that Jamie was at camp and Uncle Ken had to work but that we would all get together again soon. All get together and take the children to the beach where they could swim and build sand castles and get sand in their suits.

On the long ride Thursday afternoon to Philadelphia Carole had lots of time to think. Carole and Ernestine's father had a phrase he used to describe their mother, who always saw the potential for disaster and car wrecks and bad colds becoming pneumonia - "She can worry about a problem like a dog worries a bone." That is what Carole did on the drive. It was the first time since it happened that she had the luxury, or burden, of open hours to think about how her life had changed, so she worried it, worried all the emotional bones. "Why did he cheat do I really still love him if I really love him what does that say about me can I ever trust him again do I want him again I don't want to start over I am so mad at him I am so hurt I am so hurt I am so hurt. Or, am I mostly angry about being cheated on, being humiliated?" This went on until she couldn't stand it anymore and turned on rock and roll, loud! The fates, laughing, had the station play The Rolling Stones' You Can't Always Get What You Want followed by REO Speedwagon's Roll With The Changes. Such kidders, those fates.

Ernestine had wanted the children to be prepared for the arrival of their aunt, alone, and so had made the mistake of telling them three days early. By the time Carole got there they were bouncing off the walls, and off their parents, not "Whenarewe gonna get there" but "Whenisshe gonna get here?" Ernestine, and then Larry when he came from work, had said "In a few more hours" then "Very soon" about one hundred times that day by the time the car pulled into the driveway. Carole was gang tackled and swarmed under, worthy of any football team. It took about a half-hour for enough of the children's energy to dissipate so the adults could start to talk, except about "It," and get some food on the table.

After the children were asleep, the grown-ups settled around the white topped, red trimmed kitchen table, full from the wonderful comfort-food meal. Mugs of hot tea, blackberry. There wasn't much to say. Ernestine and Larry had the good grace to not ask exactly how she discovered them, although after talking around it for a while Carole did say "I came home earlier than they expected and caught them in the shower." What she didn't say was that, expecting it was Ken alone, she had stripped nude before making her entrance into the bathroom. There just wasn't much to say. Carole ventilated a bit, but didn't want to go through her long list of emotions and questions and emotional questions, and her loved ones weren't going to press her or offer advice since none was sought. Just as Ernestine was musing that some marriages weather the cheating storm and some do not, who can tell in advance, suddenly there was Maxwell standing in the doorway, the grownups caught guilty. But the little boy had heard nothing except a strange noise coming from his closet, maybe it sounded like something that made fire and smoke in its mouth. Larry went with him to slay the dragon and tuck Maxwell back into bed.

Chapter Four

Carole and Ernestine's parents, Smokey and Susan, live near Boston, in the house they bought between the births of their daughters. Smokey Preater's real name is Sanford, but he was called San and Sandy and others until, around the age of five, he went through a stage of being crazy about fire trucks. He owned several toy trucks, but his real love was going to the city park across from the fire station. Although fire runs were rare, there was usually one rescue run per park visit, a paramedics wagon, and Smokey was enthralled. The ultimate was a fire engine bursting from the station, or seeing one flying down a city street, siren echoing off the surrounding buildings. Childhood ecstasy. On occasions like the Fourth of July there were engines moving slowly in parades or standing in fair parking lots. Fun to look at, even touch or climb on, but the best was to see them flying by, screaming. One day he heard the term "Smoke-eater" and announced that was what he, Sanford, was, and shortly became Smokey.

Smokey lost his love of fire trucks as he grew, sports and girls taking more attention, but the name stuck, and he liked it. Eventually he became a man of exciting words, working for advertising agencies and then as a full-time consultant to companies about their advertising and marketing concepts. He retired, which actually meant that he cut down to working about two-thirds of the year for those clients he chose to keep.

Susan worked full-time as a librarian, quit for a while when the two girls were very young, and then returned part-time and stayed that way. She had other interests: an avid gardener - a love passed on to Ernestine. An enthusiastic cook - Carole's inheritance. Bridge at least twice a week - inherited by neither. Together Smokey and Sue had a fine, comfortable, part-time-employed retirement. They wanted to see their children and grandchildren but family did not consume them, busy as they were with their occupations and recreations and travels to museums and concerts in Boston, New York, and other east coast cities.

Sometimes Carole and Ernestine called to check in, sometimes their parents. This worked well for Carole now because she didn't want to say anything to them until she was ready. She decided she would call them as soon as she and Jamie got home.

Jamie was spending her third summer, two weeks each time, at the camp. It had the all-inclusive name of American Summer Camp. Tucked away in north New Jersey, away from the bustle of cars and trucks booming along highways 9 and 95 and 287, airplanes to and from Newark and the New York airports crossing overhead, traffic becomes gentler, less crowded and frantic with far fewer trucks. The scenery is better; this is one of the areas where The Garden State earns its name.

Carole continued north, turning off onto a country road, and then drove more slowly for a few miles until she saw the small wooden sign with American Summer Camp painted, of course, red white and blue. She turned onto the packed dirt and gravel road which began climbing almost immediately. As when she first brought Jamie here three years ago, Carole was again struck by how the bustle of modern civilization disappears as soon as one turns onto that dirt road. No houses or planes or cars or trucks could be seen or heard. For over a quarter mile the car climbed and wove through very thick, rich green foliage, dense underbrush with all kinds of plants and living creatures including what seemed like hundreds of mosquitoes per square foot. After that climb the road turned left and leveled off, and suddenly there was a lake down below on the left, and cabins and offices and the great hall for eating and activities straight ahead. To the right was parking, and further to the right a small meadow containing the archery range. Beyond that were horse stables that fed into small corrals and a rolling hill, almost all meadow, with riding trails. The mosquitoes were not much of a problem except at sundown, and campers and counselors and staff learned to stay in or move fast around that hour. Campfires by the lake were relatively free of them. The campfires were wonderful -- bright stars, wood smoke, roasted marshmallows, scary stories. Such a good time.

Carole had judged the time well and arrived a little ahead of the scheduled pick-up hour. She got out, stretched, and walked through the parking lot. The girls were being picked up, and cars were starting to pull in with boys for the two weeks that American would be a boy's camp. The two sexes passed each other in the parking lot or in the great hall, looking at each other or ignoring each other because of lack of interest or studiously ignoring each other because of blossoming interest. The boys would talk of girl cooties being left behind, although not all the boys. After those fierce four weeks the counselors had several days off while the camp restocked and did maintenance, and then another two weeks/ two weeks swing, this time the boys first. Two weeks later the incoming girls complained about boy cooties. The boys ranged from 8 to 14, as did the girls, and there were some reactions and facial expressions, although most wore blank faces or avoiding eyes. The parents of both sexes, dropping off tearfully/thankfully and picking up joyfully, concentrated on their own children and did not notice the brief swirl of young teen socialization.

Jamie was in the great hall, her bags packed, her brown hair secured by a headband woven during the past two weeks. It seemed to Carole that her child had leapt upward. She seemed suddenly older and taller and more on the brink of young womanhood. Jamie was tanned with a few rough sores on her arms and hands and some lesser marks on her cheeks. For a moment Jamie did not see her mother, so Carole had those seconds to admire and love and worry about her daughter, then Jamie turned and saw her and ran into her arms. They spent some minutes talking about her bug bites, the fact that they were treated with aloe and cortisone cream. "They don't itch, really Mom, don't itch." Then some goodbyes, and some more goodbyes, and buy a Dr. Pepper for the road, and load the duffel bag in the trunk. All this time Carole suffering from her own itch, her emotional itch, a need to get on the road and the conversation under way, a need to tell Jamie that her father was a total shit - no, of course not - to tell Jamie that there had been a big fight and that they were trying to work things out and not to worry.

The rehearsals, the planning while driving and with Ernestine and Larry, had been helpful. They allowed Carole to organize her thoughts, plan her words, and above all be prepared to discuss the situation calmly without tears. Jamie was talking, the radio playing softly, Jamie telling about the horses and how she really was riding better this year and maybe wanted someday to own a horse and said "Where's Dad?"

"Well, Honey, there's a problem, a rather serious problem we have to talk about."

"Is he sick?" she said with alarm.

"No, he's fine."

Jamie turned her head, looked at her mother, held the pose. Carole glanced over quickly, made eye contact, and then returned her attention to the road. "Your father and I had, not really an argument, but we are not happy with each other right now, and he's moved out. He isn't living at home, and I'm not sure how soon he will come back."

Jamie sat looking at her a long, quiet moment and then turned and looked out her window at the pine trees and suburban landscape, good homes and impressive office buildings. "Whatja fight about?"

"He isn't sure he wants to stay married. I am as surprised as you are Jamie, I thought we were doing fine but he may not want to be married any longer. I'm afraid I don't know much more, we haven't talked much since he left."

"When?"

"When did we talk or when did he leave?"

"When did Daddy move out?"

"The middle of last week."

"Where is he living, like, a hotel or something?"

"I'm not sure, he didn't tell me -- "

"So can I talk to him?"

"Of course, he is still your father." Carole heard herself say that and couldn't believe her ears. "You can call him at work tomorrow."

"When can I see him?"

"That's up to the two of you, James --- whenever you want." Jamie sat and looked out the window. Carole figured she was digesting the information, and so she just drove, listening to the radio, peeking a few times at her daughter who continued to look out the windows, turned a little away so she looked more out the side than front window. Traffic was thinning out, moving faster, heading for Boston. Soon Jamie was sound asleep, the two weeks of camping and bug bites, campfires and a bunkhouse full of giggling girls catching up to her in the comfort of the easy-riding, air-conditioned car. Carole looked over at Jamie, seeming smaller and younger and more fragile now in sleep. Carole turned down the radio a bit and thought about Ken and Jamie and -- and Sukie -- and how Jamie was going to be learning things that Carole wished would not be in her pretty, brown-haired head for another year or three or four.

Carole felt sorry for Jamie. Carole felt sorry for Carole. Carole was mad at Ken, angry mad. Whenever things were a mess, she turned to him, he to her, like normal married folks. It seemed she should go tell Ken about this problem, how upset she was. But Ken was - is - the problem, she thought. So she couldn't talk to him about it and that was terribly upsetting and frustrating -- that missing touchstone, that missing friend. The stew of emotions simmered and bubbled until, almost to her surprise, they were home.

Jamie had to be woken up. She raided the refrigerator and then watched television before again falling sound asleep. Not long after, Carole woke her grumpy and barely-awake child, made her brush her teeth and got her into bed. Carole waited for a mention of Ken, of Daddy, but there was none. Jamie was instantly asleep again, tucked in under the hand-stitched quilt given from a great aunt. Carole turned out the light, but came back to her bed and sat there watching her sleeping daughter. She shook her head in resignation and sadness as she stroked Jamie's head; but when she stirred, Carole rose quickly and left the room. Very tired, but wound up emotionally, she went back downstairs and turned on an old movie channel. Fred Astaire spun, floated magically. Carole felt sleep coming on, but fought the urge to drop off right there -- not a habit to learn, a habit she wanted to avoid. She went to bed and slept well.

Chapter Five

Carole's mother Susan, the great worrier, was always pleased and pleasantly surprised when phone calls from her children carried good news. Not that she spent hours marinating in concern, but when the phone rang she felt no surprise, almost confirmation, when the news required sympathy or even help. She and Smokey live full lives of some work -- "Keeps us young" -- and wonderful travel, east coast usually but also in recent years the Grand Canyon, Israel, and New Zealand. But there are two loved daughters, two fully approved, even loved sons-in-law, four beloved, precious grandchildren. Eight beings dear to Susan's and Smokey's hearts all moving about each day in the wicked world of car crashes, foreign terrorists, germs everywhere.

Susan's reaction to the ringing phone was dictated by the hour and the day. Nine a.m. to about eight in the evening on weekends or holidays did not startle. Weekdays the calls were not so common, so the concern factor was a bit higher. A phone ringing before nine or after eight elicited this conversation: Mother "Hello?" Either Daughter "Hi, Mom." Mother "What's Wrong?"

This was not going to be easy. Ernestine gave sympathy, love and hugs, with few questions. Details only as Carole felt like sharing. No surprise in this. The sisters had spent years building their own private latticework of rules regarding secrets – when to ask, when to share. No such latticework with their mother, of course. Carole did not want to be asked if she and Ken had been having trouble, if the marriage had been showing cracks. As far as she could tell, thinking back as well as she could remember, there were no signs of trouble. No hint that Ken was slipping away, gone away so far he could bring another woman into their marriage bed, their marriage shower where she had found them. When Ernestine and Larry talked over their tea mugs at the white kitchen table Larry asked if they had been having problems. Carole answered with one word, a soft "No -- " and shook her head slightly indicating puzzlement as much as denial, gazing down into her dark blue mug of hot brown tea. Her eyes downcast, she did not see her sister give a hard look combined with pursed lips and so slight head shake to Larry, a wife-to-husband stop sign. Larry saw the sign and stood on the brakes. That question, or any variation, was not asked again.

Of course Carole asked herself that, had asked it driving to Philadelphia and on the way to Jamie's camp. A tough question. Tough, bad choices for answers: (1) Carole as emotionally blind woman, not seeing her marriage failing and her lover leaving, missing all the warning signs, not hearing the hints, not seeing the evasion in his eyes, or (2) Carole, the self-centered, cold-hearted one, who did not examine the strength and romantic depth of her marriage as long as her needs were met – emotional, financial, sexual. Either one a stinging, blush-bringing indictment.

So now Monday morning, time to call Susan after leaving a message at work that she'd be a bit late. What to say? Head her off at Verbal Pass. "Hi, Mom, I'm afraid I have some bad news." Then quickly, against the gasp that came over the wires "No one is hurt or sick, everyone is just fine." Pause. "Ken and I had a bad fight, and he has moved out."

"Did Jamie get home from camp OK? You didn't call me yesterday, is she all right? Did she have a good time?"

Carole stood next to the counter, not choosing the comfort of the familiar kitchen stool. She stood with her head down, elbows folded in, almost as if a strong wind might pull the phone from her hand, wishing she had fortified herself with milk and cookies. She reached out with her free hand and pulled a large yellow bowl, a family favorite despite two chips and one slight crack, toward her. The bowl held apples and oranges, green and deep red grapes. Carole started picking and eating the grapes, slowly, one by one. Jamie had taken off right after breakfast to make the rounds of neighborhood friends, and likely would not be back for hours.

"Yes, Mom, she is healthy and tanned. I think she grew a couple inches, didn't get poison ivy this year, just some bug bites. Mom, you did hear what I said about Ken."

"Yes, I heard. I hope you can fix it soon, for Jamie's sake as well as yours and Ken's. Your father and I have had some tiffs over the years but he never moved out, not for one night."

A pause, during which Carole popped another grape, a green one this time, and did not yield to the urge to scream.

"How long has he been gone?"

"Almost two weeks."

Susan's voice softened way down. She said, very gently, "Oh, Honey, I'm sorry, this is really serious, isn't it? Oh dear, sweetie, I'm really sorry. What happened?"

For a strong moment Carole almost said the words, the revelation, but instead just said "It's pretty bad, Mom, but I don't want to talk about it much right now -- he says he doesn't want to be married anymore." Carole waited for the gasp, but it didn't come. Her mother truly was sad, sad for her daughter. Too upset to gasp.

Carole soon ended the conversation, promising to have Jamie call when she returned.

Later Sunday the phone rang. Carole was sure it was Ken, and it was, asking to talk to Jamie. "She's out now, probably at the Jensen's. I told her to be home by five."

"OK, I'll call about then. I'd like to take her out for dinner."

Visitation plans. Shared parenting. The first negotiations. "She may come home hungry, and I can't stand in front of the fridge waiting for you to call."

"OK, I'm at 278-5522. Please ask her to call as soon as she comes in. I can be there in about fifteen minutes."

Sure he can. Sukie's. "All right" Carole said crisply.

Ken heard her tone, guessed what she was thinking. "I'm in the Fontzen Hotel, got a furnished suite."

"A furnished suite!" Carole shook her head and hung up.

There was laundry to do. Carole washed everything, even his clothes, but after drying just stuffed his in a black plastic bag. Not petty, not vengeful, his clothes washed with the rest of the load. Not a helpmate either, nothing folded. Let Sukie deal with Ken's wrinkles.

Suddenly there was the sound of the back door opening and girls' voices and the refrigerator and cupboards being opened. Carole emerged from the laundry carrying a sturdy green plastic laundry basket with folded towels and women's and girl's garments, with a black plastic bag tied in a tight knot at the top resting on the folded items.

Jamie and the three stair-step Jensen girls, eight, nine, and just eleven, were into what was left of the milk and cookies. Time to restock. After a "Hi, girls," Carole asked Jamie to come with her for a minute. They went into Carole's room. "Jamie, your father wants to take you to supper. It's only four o'clock, I wasn't expecting you 'til five, that's what I told him. Are you still hungry after those cookies? What do you want to do, wait a while? I have his number and told him you'd call."

Jamie shrugged. She was still wearing the head band made at camp. "I only had one cookie. I dunno, five's OK, I guess."

"Well, you have to call him and tell him what time."

Jamie looked at her mother with a puzzled expression. "Mom, can I ask you something?"

"Sure, of course, always."

"Mom, you don't sound mad at him. How come you aren't

mad at him? Didn't you guys have a bad fight? He moved out and all, so--"

Carole busied her hands taking laundry out of the basket and sorting it on the bed. Jamie sat on the edge of the bed, waiting for a reply. Moving the garments aside, she sat next to Jamie and took her hands.

"Sweetness, this is going to be hard for me and for your father. If we get back together there are a lot of hurt feelings to get over. I don't want to talk much about it, but, well maybe we won't stay married." Carole shook her head "But that's not what you asked, is it?"

"No, but it's OK if you don't wanta talk about it now."

Carole leaned in a little, still holding Jamie's hands. They sat side by side on the bed, their heads turned, their faces close. Both knew this was getting into grownup stuff, emotional deep-end words.

"Yes, I am mad at him, but that is for us to fix, for me to work out. I love you very much, and Daddy loves you very much. We haven't talked about this yet but we both want to see you and be with you, and we both will. We'll work something... we'll work it out."

"If you and Daddy get divorced will I live with you?"

Carole leaned forward a few more inches, kissed her daughter's forehead and the bridge of her freckled nose. "I don't know if we are getting a divorce but I'm sure, if we do, you and I will be together. Two cool ladies."

"Can we keep living here?"

"I tell you the truth, right?"

"Right."

"OK, truth. Truth is I don't know. I mean, we might fix everything and this will just be a bad time we got through. If not -- well, if not I can only do probably. Probably we'll stay here, you and me. Not ninety-nine percent, but pretty probably. Now, you have three guests to send home, and a father to call. Please don't worry, really really please don't worry. We both love you to pieces, and that won't change. Here's the number. Go."

Jamie left to rejoin the girls who had resourcefully popped microwave popcorn and settled in front of the television. Jamie grabbed a handful of popcorn, said "You guys, my dad's coming soon, yulhafta go then" and headed for the kitchen phone.

Carole finished putting away her clothes, then took Jamie's into her daughter's bedroom and placed the folded clothes on the bed for Jamie to put away. Back in her room, she saw the plastic bag and suddenly realized that she didn't want him in the house. What to do? Carole went into the kitchen just as Jamie was hanging up. "He'll behere in fifteen minutes."

"Fine. Look, honey, I'll put this bag by the door, it has some of your dad's clothes in it. Watch for him and take it out and give it to him when he comes, OK?"

Carole thought about the best way to avoid him. Taking a shower might work, might really feel good, but the irony was too great. She decided just to join Jamie and the Jensen contingent, share the few remaining kernels, and watch what was left of a TV show about teenage detectives who outsmarted the bad guys and helped the confused police. The detectives wore wonderful, teenage-trendy clothes. The show's sponsor sold wonderful, teenage-trendy clothes.

Carole's worrying was not necessary; Ken tapped his horn in the driveway, Jamie jumped up with a "There's Dad" and was gone, taking the black plastic bag with her to the car. The Jensens stayed until the bad guys were jailed and then left, saying thanks for the popcorn and the milk and cookies. Good kids. Carole took a shower, washed her hair, and put on a robe, her hair wrapped in a terrycloth turban. She ate some fruit and cheese, and then, teased by the small amount she had earlier, made a bowl of microwave popcorn all for herself.

Soon after the horn sounded, Jamie ran out dragging the black plastic bag behind her, catching it on the door. She turned, got it on her back, and started down the front walk. Ken got out of his car, half ran to her and grabbed her up in his arms, bag and all. "Hey, Princess, I have missed! You!"

"Hi, Daddy. Mommy sent some clothes to you."

"Oh, that's the bag. Here, give it to me and I'll put it in the trunk."

"Don't forget like the doughnuts."

The doughnuts were a family memory, a bag bought before a vacation and then forgotten in a corner of the trunk behind a box; when finally discovered they were sprouting interesting colors.

Ken threw the bag in trunk where, screened from the house in case Carole was watching, he quickly untied the knot and inspected. Clean, dry clothes. "Thanks, Carole," he thought, a little surprised.

Jamie was in the car, buckling in, and had turned the key so the radio would come on. She found her favorite station, a constant parade of music aimed at an under-18 audience, with advertisements to match. Jamie was singing along with a recording by a breathy teenage girl, backed by electronically perfect percussion.

Ken got in, gave the parental pro forma request for a lower volume, and pulled out of the driveway. He avoided glancing at the house, at the windows.

"So howcum you and Mom had a fight? She said you might not fix it, she didn't know about you cummin back home. Are you guys gettingadivorce?"

"Do I get to ask you about camp or do we have to do the grownup stuff first?"

"Well, I made this head band, lots cool, right?" she said, turning her head so he could see.

"Nice. You sure you didn't buy it at the camp store? It looks very professional."

"Daddy" she exclaimed, slapping his arm.

He laughed and said "And what else?"

"Well, yuhknow I went there last year. Same things, horses, crafts, campfires, 'bouta bazillion mosquitoes. OK food."

Ken turned, looked at her, his wonderful daughter. He hoped they could stay good friends. "Any girls from last year?"

"A girl named Kellie. She was in my bunk last year, and this year, and a coupla others. So when do we getta talk about you about you and Mom?"

Ken sighed, a small, brief sound. "Only one more, I promise. Where do you want to go eat? You choose. Tell you what. As soon as we are settled at the eating place I'll tell you all about -- well, I won't tell you all about it, but lots, and no changing the subject."

As he guessed she would, Jamie chose a pleasant neighborhood place, a white, wood frame restaurant on a corner in a residential area. Stannarz is known for its juicy hamburgers and great french fries and thick, real ice cream milkshakes. Jamie chose all three: burger with mustard ketchup extra pickles, fries, chocolate shake. Ken chose the 10 ounce strip steak, medium, baked potato with sour cream, and coffee. He got a promise from Jamie for a taste of her milkshake.

They were sitting in a booth, red fake leather fabric on the back and seats; easily cleaned, stain resistant. Ken laced his fingers together and looked at his daughter.

"OK, my favorite princess, do I get to make a little speech first or right into the questions:"

"Daddy, you promised."

"Yes I did. And question the first is?"

"What did you fight about?"

Ken had not only rehearsed this, but had talked to his lawyer, who had offered a few words of advice but strongly urged the services of a counselor who specializes in divorce and children of divorce. Ken had not taken that step yet, although he was prepared to if things turned sour. Ken also purchased three books on the stress of divorce on children and maintaining ties and similar subjects. He had read parts of all three.

"You aren't the same person that you were five years ago. Neither am I. I met your mother about fifteen years ago, a long time. We have been married for thirteen years. Now I know some people, like your grandma and grandpa Preater, have been married lots more years, almost forty. That is wonderful. I think it really is wonderful, I mean it, that your grandma and grandpa are still married, and the same for everyone else like that. Someday you will get married, after you get three college degrees and start our own business, after that --" Jamie was peeling the paper off two straws in anticipation of her milkshake. She made a face at him but said nothing.

"Really, Honey, my deepest wish for you, aside from the excellent use you make of your brain and talent, is a long, forever marriage. Happily ever after, like the stories all end. But I haven't answered your question, have I?"

"No, Daddy, you haven't, and I've got lots more."

Ken laughed. "Onward, then, it is. Answer: I changed. I don't know why. There is no one to blame. Your mother is a fine woman." He shook his head. "I can do that better. Like this. Your mother is a very nice person, a good, kind, intelligent woman, a wonderful mother. I like her. I don't love her. I don't want us to be married, don't want to be married to her anymore. Lots of don'ts, hey?"

Ken waited for a response, or question, but there was none. A silence stretched during which Jamie played with her straws and the discarded wrappers, picking them up by using the straws as pincers. Ken guessed she needed time to absorb his words so he let the moment lengthen. The waiter appeared with their orders, and they both ate heartily for a few minutes.

"So you're not mad at Mom."

"Not at all, nothing to be mad about."

"But she said you had a fight."

"OK, now I understand, you think it was a fight like two people are so mad they are screaming at each other." Jamie nodded, eagerly working the french fries. "We fought about what I said, about not staying married. Your mom wants to stay married, and I don't, so we don't agree, but I am not mad at her."

"But she is mad atchu."

"Geshunthiet."

"Daddy! Maddddd atttt youuuuu."

"Yes, fairy princess, she is mad at me. Yes she is, and I don't blame her. But I'm not mad at her."

"Sonow what happens?" Jamie was making rapid progress through her meal, despite the fact that every single french fry had to be dunked and smeared in a small hill of ketchup until only the part where her fingers held it lacked a ketchup coating.

"Who does what next?"

"Yeah, like that."

"Well, I can't tell you -- can't be sure my answer would be the same as your mother's. Except for one thing, and that is we both love you and want you to be as happy as possible whatever we work out."

"She said that too." Jamie suddenly stopped eating, dropped her hands at her sides, looked down and lifted the hand with the ketchup-speckled fingers, grabbed several paper napkins and cleaned her fingers and the spot she had just created on the booth seat. She worked busily on them, no looking at her father.

"I'm madatchu."

No father humor this time. "Why?"

"Because I don't want you to go, don't want Mommy to be alone or us to be alone. I'm scared. I miss you at home. I don't want us to do this."

Having finished her lecture, Jamie returned to her meal, but at a slower pace. She was sad of face, not crying but still not looking at him.

Ken took the foil off his baked potato. He always ate the skin. "Honey," he said softly, "I don't want you to be scared of anything. There is nothing to be afraid of."

Jamie looked up, made a face at him.

"Very stupid?"

"Very stupid!"

"Talking to you like a child?"

Again the all-encompassing "Daddy!" but this time accompanied by a smile.

"All right, more grownup. Seriously. Tell me what you are afraid of or worried about and I will try to answer you so you won't be anymore."

Jamie resumed eating. Ken took a spoonful of her milkshake, pronounced it yummy, then Jamie finished off the drink with a flourish, loud sounds from the bottom of the glass. "If you get divorced where will I live?"

Ken's attorney had told him what a reasonable expectation was. Their county's courts were concerned about and protective of the interests of any children in a divorce. Mediation of parenting agreements was mandated; the court wouldn't proceed with a divorce unless an agreement for sharing time and at least basic expenses was presented. Sometimes these mediations proceeded smoothly, with both parents cooperating and, on occasion, yielding, with an agreement reached in a few productive sessions. This was rare, as was the opposite: two people so bloody angry with each other that they could not be in the same room. Those angry mediations, involving the attorneys as well as the parents and lots of back and forth phone calls and relayed messages took much longer and burned up a lot of dollars in legal fees, but the eventual result was nearly the same. The parents presented to the court a plan for raising their children, holidays and vacations and school and money, of course money. Most journeys to agreements were somewhere in the middle: tears, raised voices, but not too many nor too long. A few hours with attorneys checking back on the agreements reached in mediation, but usually after six to eight hours in the mediator's office an agreement was ready to be put in legal language and made part of the divorce settlement.

Ken had already decided that if Carole wanted to provide the primary home for Jamie, the home for the school year, that was fine with him. He had seen the standard divorce agreement, the model offered by the court, and it worked well for his needs. Ken had no idea how long this thing, this sex fling with Sukie, would last but it sure wasn't going to end in marriage. In fact, he had already moved out of her house, by mutual agreement. Sukie viewed him in turn as a sex fling, and wanted to keep her options open, so when he said the first night that he would get a place the next day or two she smiled and said she looked forward to visiting him there. For now he was in a hotel that rented small suites by the week or month, but he had not decided where he would live; somewhere near Boston of course, because he had no intention of quitting his job. In fact, maybe downtown. He had never lived downtown in a big city, and it might be fun -- bright lights, great restaurants, theaters, beautiful women. Not a residential area suitable for Jamie, but he wanted a place for her to visit, to stay, not a place to live. He remembered there would be the legal cost of divorce, probably child support, maybe a settlement on the house. Better be moderate on the beautiful downtown women.

"Well, if we get divorced -- no, wait. I want to say that differently. I don't think we are going to stay together, your mother and I. So how about I say 'when,' because I think that is the truth. So, when we get divorced you will probably live most of the time, almost all the school year, with your mother. And I think it will be in the house you are in now, if I can guess one of your next questions." Jamie nodded, finishing off the last of her meal. "Do you know what the word 'equity' means?"

"No."

"Good word for you to learn. Use it next year in school and dazzle your teacher."

The waiter appeared, a lanky teenager with the big feet

and hands of a basketball front-court man. He politely asked if they wanted anything else, put down the check when both Jamie and her father said no, and cleaned up all the dishes at once, scooping them up in a quick, sure motion. Good hands.

"Equity means the value in something that is the worth, the cash worth, in it. Bad English. Let me try again. Simple example. Let's say you bought a house for -- small numbers. Monopoly money. Let's say you bought a house for ten dollars, paid five down and owed the bank five."

"Daddy, you can't owe the bank in Monopoly."

"Well yes, but, never mind. Just go with the example. House worth ten, paid five, your equity, your cash worth is five even though the house is worth ten because--"

"Because I still owe half the ten."

Ken smiled broadly, proud father. "Atta girl! Now do this. You have a house worth ten, paid five, your equity is five. Now I come along and say that I love your house, want to buy it. I know you paid ten. I will pay you twelve because I love the way you painted it. OK, so you say yes. If you sell and I buy, what is your equity?"

She paused only a moment. "So, I owe five, you will give me twelve - I have your twelve, go to the bank and give them their five, and I have seven. So the answer is seven, right?"

"Exactly right, my mathematical princess. There are some wrinkles like taxes and the cost of that paint you used and other stuff, but you have the picture. So, we have a house, that is, your mother and I have a house. We have a mortgage, that's like the five you still owed the bank. We have equity, money we paid when we bought the house, like you paid five for a house worth ten and owed the rest. We have equity in the house, both money we have paid and money, extra money value, because it is worth more now than the day we bought it. So we, and the bank, could figure the equity. Now what happens?"

Jamie slid quickly out of the booth. "Now what happens is you take me to the park and buy me some ice cream."

"Ice Cream! You just had a milk shake!"

"I'm growing, Daddy, I need lots of food. Do you want me to starve?"

They drove to the park, bubble gum music popping on the radio. They arrived and sat in sling seat swings, giant swings with ten-foot chains. They both swung high, even to the point where the swing stalls and you feel like you are falling. It scared Ken more than Jamie, and the recent dinner spoke to him from his belly, so he quit swinging, got up and walked to a nearby bench. Jamie swung a little more, then came and got him and they went to the concession stand, leased from the city by the same family for twenty-seven years, two generations. Jamie with enthusiasm and Ken with trepidation bought vanilla chocolate swirl soft ice cream cones, his small, hers medium, then found another bench nearby, a green wooden one, part of a circle of benches about forty feet across. In the center of the circle was a cement fountain with water bubbling up from the drinking spout in the middle and a faucet on the side for filling bottles.

"Can I talk about the house just a little more?"

"Sure, I like you talking to me like this."

"I'm glad you like. So here it is. Two people, Ken and Carole, own a house. They decide to split up. They both have equity. No, they both share in the equity in the house. Remember the ten dollar house?"

Jamie nodded, working the cone hard. He marveled at her appetite.

"What probably will happen is that Ken, that's me, Ken," she was too busy to make a face at him, trying to keep ahead of the cone's melt rate, "-- will sell his half of the house, and the equity, his half of the equity, to Carole. So instead of me owning half and Mommy owning half, she buys it and owns it all."

"But how does she pay you?" Without waiting for the answer, she said "Hold this, please" and thrust the cone at him. She ran to the fountain and drank and washed around her mouth and got water from the faucet for her hands and sort of washed them and shook them dry, finishing the job on her jeans. Waiting for her return, Ken finished his smaller cone and, when she returned, gave hers back and headed for the fountain. Then she needed another turn at the bubbling water.

They sat on the bench, a bit too warm but too full of their meal and their soft ice cream cones and water to move just yet.

Ken stretched, yawned, raised his hands over his head. A nap would feel wonderful. "'bout ready to go home?"

"No, Daddy, you have to answer the question first."

He looked blank for a moment, then said "Oh yes, how does Mommy pay me? Lots of ways, but here's two. She has a good job. Your mother has a good job, gets a good salary. So one way is she goes to a bank and asks them to pay me, just pay me off. Then she pays them back, some each month. Another is no bank, she just pays me. Sends me checks each month. And other options, ideas. But whatever way we go, she ends up owning the house."

Ken waited for Jamie to ask about visits, vacations, time with her father, but she was suddenly tired, yawning like he did. Perhaps tired of the subject, the conversation. He took her home, hugged and kissed her in the car before she got out. As he drove away he thought "That wasn't so bad."

Chapter Six

"Ken, I want to talk."

"About Jamie?"

"No, well, yes, about Jamie, and us, our family. Are you going to be -- were you going to call me?"

"I did call, I tried to talk to you about us. You hung up."

"I hung up because, without one word, one single word of apology or regret you just tell me to get a lawyer."

Ken rubbed his face, a familiar gesture. "I hate doing this over the phone. I'm not sure I am saying it right, or you are hearing it right. Can I come over tomorrow?"

"Can you come over, can you come over?" Carole said, her voice rising and tightening. "It's your house! Why are you acting this way?"

"I don't think Jamie should be there. What time do you want me?"

It was at that moment, that exact moment, Carole fully realized her marriage of more than thirteen years was terribly sick, maybe already over. It was certainly more than a broken vow of fidelity. He wanted to visit his former residence, his already former wife, to work things out. As he had said, "to cut a good deal." There was no love in his voice, no regret or yearning, just efficient problem solving.

"Seven. Jamie won't be there. Goodbye."

Carole got up, left her cubicle, wandered into the break

room. It was empty except for three administrative assistants who were taking a mid-morning break at one of the tables. Actually it was a non-smoking break. They had made a pledge to be strong, the three of them, and forever kick the habit as three against the enemy. Forced by habit, one of them clicked open her purse and started to put her hand inside, reaching for the cigarettes not there. "I really want to stop doing that," she said with a small laugh while the other two shook their heads and smiled in sympathetic understanding. Then their microwave popcorn finished popping and they opened the bag and attacked.

Carole bought a can of apple juice, picked up a straw, looked at the array of snacks but none appealed. She sat down at a table on the far side of the room from the popcorn eaters and thought. It was not a logical sequence but rather several voices, speaking truths and beliefs, offering up their wisdom. First, Ken is gone. She knew him, his voice, moods, decision followed by action. Not a woman's but a wife's intuition. Break of heart. Pit of stomach. Ken is gone.

At the same time, other contending thoughts were present for consideration. One big obvious truth was that her intuition hadn't told her he was fucking someone. "Making Love" didn't apply to Sukie.

Carole was fooled. She was fool. So maybe her heart and tummy were wrong to be so certain of the end. Still another voice insisted, certain or not, she had to try to save the marriage. No, not had to, wanted to. She was pissed beyond belief, one of her father's favorite phrases, but she had no doubt she wanted Ken and would take him back. Counseling, of course. And a long time before sex. But while the picture of him yearning for her, doing penance, sounded good, the first voice - pit of stomach and core of heart - restated flatly that was vain fantasy. Ken is gone. Carole finished her apple juice, threw away the straw, rinsed the can and put it in the aluminum recycling bin. She went back to work and focused on the tasks, hard on the computer keyboard and deep into the paperwork.

Carole told Jamie that her father was coming over after dinner the next night so that they, Ken and Carole, could have a serious talk. "We need privacy, honey, and we don't want to go to a bar or restaurant. So I am asking you to please understand and give us some time tomorrow. I'll call Mrs. Jensen or Mrs. Kowchin or anyone else you want. I'm sorry to ask you to leave for a while, really I am."

"It's OK, Mom. What if the Kowchins wannago to a movie, kinigo too?"

"Smooth, clever daughter. Wasn't that Debbie Kowchin you were talking to earlier? Did she say they were going to a movie tomorrow?"

For once Jamie slowed her rapid-fire delivery. "You are just the smartest mom, just the greatest most generous, smartest mom."

Carole took up her daughter in her arms, laughing, been a while since she had a good laugh. She kissed and squeezed the child a moment, laying her cheek against Jamie's forehead. "I love you, clever daughter. Do you want me to call Mrs. Kowchin?"

"No, Debbie and me'll fix it."

"Debbie and I will fix it. You cannot be president of the United States if you make grammatical errors."

"Not gonnabe, Mom. I'm gonna marry--"

"Please, for me, going to."

Making a face, slowing for dramatic effect, "I am going to marry a rich man and sit home all day and eat ice cream."

Carole sighed. "If you must, but it will be our nation's loss."

"Mom!" Jamie broke away and went to call Debbie. She returned a moment later and asked "When is Dad coming, what time?"

"Seven, why?"

"They want to pick me up about seven, and I wondered if he'd be here so I could see him."

"Well, he was planning on seven, but you could call and ask him to come a bit early."

As soon as Carole said it she regretted it, although it was the right thing to say to Jamie. The idea of Ken being in the house, chatting and laughing with Jamie, while both adults waited for her to leave so they could get to the hard discussion sounded miserable. "On the other hand," debating the thoughts in conflict, "he may realize he misses being home with his family." "Nonsense!" came the quick opposing thought.

As it turned out the situation was not so stressful. Jamie opened the door for her father while Carole finished cleaning up from supper, and she stayed at the kitchen counter working on a shopping list. Bits of conversation came her way, mostly Jamie's speedy word delivery, about movies seen and to be seen and neighborhood friends. Soon the Kowchin's car was in the driveway and Jamie quickly kissed both parents and ran out the door.

The car pulled away and the married couple sat where they were, Ken on the couch, not his usual spot, sitting as if patiently waiting in the dentist's office. Carole sat not twenty feet away, separated from him by a wall with a barely started list – eggs, milk, toothpaste – and some coupons on the counter before her. For the second time Carole heard that voice of certain reason, solid as a wall of rock, that her marriage was over. He wouldn't even call out her name. Carole took a deep breath, put down her pen and slowly got up from the chair and walked into the living room. As she did, she thought that this is how unexpected domestic violence erupts. Like the quick opening of a furnace door, all the shame humiliation anger hurt fear roared, the searing heat suddenly on face and chest. But on the outside, for Ken's view, only cool.

Cool she was. As she walked into the living room Carole was ice lady. She sat across from him, sat on the front edge, then in a moment back in the chair. He looked at her with the most neutral look she had ever seen. She waited.

Now Ken came forward, sitting upon the edge of the couch cushions. His face suddenly softening, he opened his hands toward her. "Carole, I have been a real jerk, and I'm sorry. I should not have had another woman in our place. I should have sat down with you and told you how I feel. I'm truly sorry to have shocked you like that." He paused, dropped his hands. It was clearly her turn to speak. Carole could feel the audience turn towards her, watching this tale of two endings - end of love, end of marriage. Well, the audience and director would just have to wait. Ken had rehearsed his lines, she had not. Carole was aware he had apologized for sex in their bed, not for the sex. She took a breath, started a careful response.

"And now what, Kenneth? You want me to forgive you and we build anew? You want me to understand and let's call the lawyers and get it over with? I'm not sure where we are," said the ice lady, controlled voice.

Ken got up. For a tiny moment she thought he was coming to her – bended knee! But instead he just made a circle, walked once around the room, a curious movement. When he got back to the starting point he stopped and faced her, still standing. His voice was strained, strange. "I don't want to be married. I feel your emotional needs like a weight and that isn't fair to you because you really don't ask much of me. But I just -- don't want -- to be married. This thing with Sukie is just sex. You know I'm not living with her."

She gave him an ice lady stare. "Ken, sit down, will you? Please!"

He sat down. "I don't know, this isn't going the way I planned."

"Tell me what you planned. What were my lines? What was I supposed to say? You know, you said you wanted to come over and talk, but really you wanted to set up a discussion and have it go according to a plan in your head. I am so mad right now I'm not sure I want to continue this at all."

"Look, I know I'm stumbling around, but I really want to talk to you about this -- and that means hearing what you want to say. I'll listen."

"Listen to what? I don't -- what did you want -- what did you think we were going to say to each other?"

Ken rocked forward to allow his hand to extract a handkerchief from a back pocket. He wiped his eyes and nose, taking several moments, then replaced the cloth. "I planned on saying what I did. I want a fair divorce, one that is good for us, fair to you and Jamie."

"Oh shit, Ken, good for us?"

"No, maybe just fair. I want to do the right thing -- things -- financially, and I am only asking that you not poison Jamie Sue against me. I want to see Jamie and be her father. I hope we can agree on that. I want to -- enough. What do you say?"

"What do I say. Let's see. Where is the emphasis? You would like to hear 'What do I say, meaning do I accept your offer of a fair divorce, right now, do the deal, get it done, figure out what to do about Jamie," her voice rising sharply and the words coming faster and faster. "But I think I'll choose this one, 'what do *I* say'. And what I say is that there are no deals, no lawyers, at least until we try counseling. It may be a waste of time," jaw ever tighter "But I'll tell you, Kenneth Tagee, you're a mess. You're a mess and I'm confused and I want us to go talk to someone."

"To fix me. To bring me to my senses."

They looked at each other for a moment.

"Perhaps, Ken. Or perhaps to help me understand. Accept. Cope. You owe me that."

Ken stood, his posture indicating he was leaving. "What have you told Jamie?"

Carole leaned back in her chair, held the chair's arms in her hands, shook her head a bit and blinked. "Did I miss something? Did we just turn a corner? You owe me a visit to a counselor, maybe two, maybe more, I don't know." Her voice was getting louder, the anger returning. "I repeat, you owe me that, owe me a try with a counselor. You didn't answer but started talking about Jamie. Answer the question!"

"Question being will I go to a counselor with you? The answer is yes, one time. I will not make a promise about more -- any more visits – sessions -- whatever in the hell they call them. And I'm asking about Jamie because I've been doing some reading and she is just too damn young to cope with infidelity, especially her parents." Seeing Carole's eyes widen, he held up his hands and said "Father! Father unfaithful, not parents. She doesn't need that in her head yet. So, what have you told her?"

"Just that we had a bad fight. No divorce talk. Certainly no infidelity talk, do you think I'm stupid?"

He looked at her, looked right into her eyes, and said in a softer, somewhat sad voice, "No, Carole, you are certainly not stupid. Jury is still out on me. I'll block out some days, or parts of days, and email them to you. You schedule the counselor and I'll be there." He walked to the door and started to open it, then said with his back to her, "Thank you about Jamie," and left.

Chapter Seven

Dr. Ckeye was a thin, elegant woman in her seventies, or perhaps eighties. She moved, not as much slowly as carefully, inviting them into her office, shaking hands firmly with Ken and Carole and asking them to take a seat. The doctor wore her hair tied back with a velvet bow that coordinated with her proper, tailored suit. Her office was large, with one wall almost full of books. Everything was well-worn leather, beautiful dark woods, comfortable wing chairs, and a desk in the corner that was an antique dealer's dream. A beautiful, comfortable, wonderful office.

Two chairs, with a small table between, faced one chair. The two were identical, and the table between held a rose in a crystal bud vase and a small box of tissues. There was also a small carafe and two empty, bright-clean glasses. Under the table was a tiny, empty wastebasket. Dr. Ckeye's wing chair was a brighter brocade than the two it faced, and her table held a small pad and bronze colored ballpoint pen, a carafe and one glass.

All the financial and insurance papers had been filled out in the outer office. Ken and Carole had been told what to bring and to be there at 2:00 with the appointment to begin at 2:30. Ken, who strongly believes people should be on time, noted that the doctor opened her office door for them at 2:24.

Dr. Ckeye picked up her pen and pad, and looked at them

with astonishingly bright, turquoise eyes. "Carole, Ken" she said, looking directly at each in turn, "Please tell me why we are here."

Ken began. "I don't want to be here, no offense, Dr. Ckeye, but you are a marriage counselor, and I don't want to be counseled. I'm not trying to save this marriage, Carole is. I won't change my mind."

The slightest shrug. The doctor's voice was soft but clear. "But you came so that--"

"Carole insisted. I feel like I have to do this so we can get on with it."

"The divorce."

"Yes."

Dr. Ckeye turned her head, her shoulders just a little. Carole noticed that the doctor's legs were crossed at the ankle. "Carole?"

"I thought about this, about why I wanted to come. OK, first, I am hurt and angry. He was unfaithful to me. In our bed. I am very hurt. He doesn't begin to understand what he has done to me." A long pause. "I love him." Another pause, a ragged breath. Ken sat looking at Dr. Ckeye, not at his wife. "I am very mad, very hurt, angry, insulted, angry -- I want, here is what I want. Two things. I want to be sure, both of us to be sure, that it is over. And if we both are sure, then I guess I need some advice, because I sure don't want to be in love with Ken if he isn't in love with me. I don't want that." Carole could feel the tears almost starting, but she raised her chin and arched her eyebrows high and tight and talked on, quickly. "So I want to hear him tell me that. I heard him say 'I love you' enough times, I guess I want him to tell me he doesn't."

"And the second thing?"

"Why. Just why. Why?"

"Please, why what?"

"Uhh, everything, all. Why did he have sex with another woman? Why does he want a divorce? Why won't he try to save our marriage? Why?"

"Please, Carole" Ken said, turning to look at her. "I am still sorting things out, but I really know I don't want to go on with this. I want you to get a lawyer. I want us to be decent to each other and get on with our lives. Maybe I'm sorry I came here because I don't want you thinking I will change my mind. You know, Carole, that's just the point, and I've told you that a dozen times."

"What is the point?"

"That my mind is changed. I have changed. I don't want to be married anymore. Over and over I keep saying these things, and I'm tired of saying them. I'm not coming back here, or doing more counseling. I did this for you. I guess I should have refused."

"And you don't think I deserve to know why." A statement.

"People fall in love, people are in love, they fall out -- they fall out of love, they go on to the next thing. Some people stay forever, and that is great. Maybe I'm jealous of them, I don't know, but that's not me or what happened to me. I fell in and I fell out and here we are. What do you want from me?"

"My goodness, Kenneth" Carole said, not looking at him. "You sound like an acrobat, in and out and on to the next. Or maybe a rabbit."

"Doctor Ckeye, I'd like to ask something."

"Certainly, Ken...you prefer Ken."

"Yes."

"Certainly, Ken, this is for you and Carole."

"Doctor, I feel like I am being blackmailed. I know my mind, and I have been thinking about Carole and our marriage and -- and sex and other women and getting divorced. I have been thinking about it all for some time now. Carole knows, she can tell you, I am a planner, a muller. Well, I have mulled this plenty, including how it will affect our daughter Jamie. And the fact that I will see less of Jamie, who knows, she may even hate me for a while. But that's for Jamie and me to figure out. As for Carole, well, I'm not going nuts, not doing the mid-life crises thing. Bit young for that, anyway. Carole keeps acting as though I need to be cured or something. You know, come to my senses. The truth is, Doctor --" He paused, turning towards his wife.

"The truth is, Carole, that I want to make this change, don't want to continue, oh, what, continue down this road. I'm not mad at you, I don't hate you," shrugging "I don't love you. There. Said. I'm asking what you want, money, what, so I can go away. Shit, Carole, I just want to go away. Let me go."

"Is it Sukie?"

"No, it isn't, and you aren't listening to me at all. I'm sorry, but this is not only a waste of time, but now it is getting insulting. I know what I'm doing, I realize I have hurt you, I want a divorce, I will work out a fair settlement, and --. Look, damn it, damn it all to hell. I don't want to hurt you but you keep making me say it. I don't love you anymore. I did, and I don't. Want it in writing?"

"Ken, Carole, I would like to spend some time speaking to each of you separately for a few minutes. Carole, if it is acceptable to you, I'd like to start with Ken."

Carole nodded, rose from her chair, head high, opened the door, went through and closed it gently. There were no magazines but today's newspaper in the waiting room, and the last few days' papers in a rack against a wall. She had not noticed when they sat in this room earlier while filling out the insurance forms, but the walls held several fine paintings of flower gardens, quaint cottages, and seascapes. There were also four small frames containing calligraphy on parchment.

"The way to love anything is to realize it might be lost." G. K. Chesterton.

"You cannot make yourself feel something you do not feel, but you can make yourself do right in spite of your feelings." Pearl S. Buck.

"Don't compromise yourself. You are all you've got." Janis Joplin.

"How often we are offended by not being offered something we do not really want." Eric Hoffer.

Carole stood and read the Hoffer statement three times, then turned away and sat in one of the comfortable chairs.

Carole suddenly felt so tired. It occurred to her that Ken could just do his steady resolve thing until he wore her down. If the marriage was in fact over she had to know, wanted both of them to come to that through clear understanding, not resigned weariness. Maybe she would have to say that she accepted the sad truth, but she didn't want to say "You win, I give up, I'm too tired." And she wanted to know why.

In the office the sun had moved since they had arrived, and now came through the window and shown hard on a picture of Dr. Ckeye with Roselyn Carter. Ken wanted no extra words, and did not ask about it.

"Ken, I want to say that I am here to help both you and Carole to get to a place where you are at peace, where you can get on with your lives. Not just get on, but be happy, be healthy. That place you may reach as a couple or after separation. I am not here to advocate any point of view or any life decision, although I am opposed to divorce and do try to save marriages, especially when there are children. But whatever the outcome, I am here to advocate making as calm and well-reasoned decisions as possible, hard for most people to do when they are in emotional pain. I advocate stepping back, looking carefully, being sure, and never forgetting the interests of the children.

He looked at her a long moment, and she waited, unmoving. What an elegant, refined lady. "Doctor, I have to tell you, I came here -- well, I said it. It seemed like blackmail, but it's really hard to be angry at you."

"Angry because?"

"No good reason, not at you I guess, but at the system, the 'get fixed' system -- but that's not what you are doing. I understand, I really appreciate what you just said." Another pause, long pause. Waiting time, a counselor's good friend.

Ken opened his hands, palms up, a questioning look. "Now what?"

"You say you don't love Carole, that you don't want to be married, and you sound very sure. May I ask you when you discovered you didn't love her?"

The deep, long sigh. "A long time ago, I don't know, more than a -- no, more than two years. I liked her, still do, really like her, but something went away. Or went out. Anyway, there I was -- want to know when it first really hit me?"

"Please."

"We were making love, and I suddenly realized that the, the -- I don't know what to call it -- the warm love feeling was gone. I was just screwing her. We weren't making love -- I guess, I guess for me, we weren't -- I am having trouble explaining this."

"You are doing very well. Your meaning is clear: having sex, not making love."

"Yes, exactly."

"And you felt that this was -- "

"Well, it stayed that way. We were making -- having sex once or twice a week, and I enjoyed it, but then I would think the next morning that I didn't love her, that I had to get out of the relationship. I had that discussion with myself every single morning after we did it, every time, for more than a year. I would say to myself, 'I've got to get out of this relationship.' That phrase, in the shower, or shaving. 'I've got to get out of this relationship.' I liked -- do today like -- her, but I'm just not in love with the woman I married."

"And Sukie?"

"People flirt, Doctor. That came out wrong, sorry, you know that. But, well, people flirt, usually never meaning it most times, I guess. She flirted, I flirted back, she kept it up, I said I mean it, she said she did too, and we were in bed the next day. And it was good, and I want more, and I don't want to hurt Carole anymore. I don't love her. I want other women, and -- and -- enough?"

"This is not a test, Ken. You describe your feelings and experiences well. You seem to know what you want. Many couples come to me to save their marriages. They have lots of problems, astounding, terrible problems, but they both want, to some extent, to save it. Usually one wants to more than the other, but they want to try or they wouldn't be here. You, as I understand, don't want to save your marriage to Carole. You are here as part of the process, a step she insisted upon. Correct?"

"Well, yes, but I'm sure she wants to fix me -- wants you to fix me."

Dr. Ckeye sat a small moment, and then said, "Please trade places with Carole, Ken. It will be a short visit, and then I will ask you to join us."

Carole sat down and looked at the wise older woman, so calm and sure. It seemed that there should be a teapot nearby, and for the doctor to ask her to pour.

"Carole, I am here to counsel people on their marital problems, to help heal the marriage, to fend off the divorce dragon if I can. I cannot make anyone love anyone. I cannot rekindle a flame. If the marriage isn't saved, sometimes I can help heal the broken heart -- help one, or even both, get well and strong again. That is what I can do, and what I can't."

Carole, flat, without emotion. "So my marriage is over."

Dr. Ckeye did not respond.

"I don't know what to do, don't know the -- the rules. Here I was married, thought I'd be married forever, married to Ken. Suddenly I feel like I'm in Sri Lanka or on the moon. Everything is upside down. I'm dealing with things I never planned, never thought I would have to worry over. Too damn many emotions --"

"Say something about those emotions."

"A list? Angry, very angry, hurt, scared, lonely, insulted, confused. Why? Why? I keep asking Ken that, and all I get is, 'It just happened' or 'People fall in love people fall out of love' or 'It is not about you.' My head spins. I can't feel them all at the same time so they take turns running things, running me -- sort of king of the hill of my emotions. And all the while I have to go to work and not run any red lights and be as normal as possible in front of Jamie so I don't scare her. What a confusing mess."

A small smile from Dr. Ckeye. "Confusing in Sri Lanka."

"Yes, or here on moon."

A pause.

"Ken has said that he is not coming back. Unless he changes his mind, we won't be together again, that is, the three of us. I am available to you, and to him, if I can help either one of you sort out your thoughts or be comfortable with yourselves. But that is for later. For today, I don't know what else we can do, do you?"

Carole looked down at her hands, flat in her lap. She raised them and opened them wide, spreading her fingers, palms down, rolled her shoulders, trying to ease the terrible weight crushing down. "No, nothing. I guess I have to learn how to -- ah, live on the moon." Her turn for a slight smile. She sat up straight, and said with forced brightness "Yep! I have to learn how to be a divorced woman. A divorced woman. Marital status? Divorced. Will you help me?"

Although the doctor's voice had been gentle throughout the sessions, it became a touch softer. "I can help you to find ways to feel good about yourself, to be as happy as possible, which in time should be just happy, no 'as possible' appended. I can help you get on with your life. But my role is only to clarify, to assist you in exploring your feelings and finding your path, your own path, not one I point out. You do most of the work, not me -- I'm a clarifier, not a teacher. If you want that, I would be pleased to help."

Carole nodded, and Dr. Ckeye continued, normal voice resumed. "I would like to bring Ken back now."

Carole nodded again, a small motion, and the doctor went to the door, opened it, and asked Ken to join them.

"Here is what I understand from what you both have shared with me. Ken, you've said you don't want to seek a reconciliation, but would rather end your marriage in a non-adversarial manner. You want out of the marriage, but you're not angry with her and don't want to be mean. From that I assume you don't want to hurt Carole emotionally, financially or personally any more than can be helped. Am I correct?"

"Yes, and -- yes. Yes."

"Carole, you would like to see if your marriage can be saved, and such saving would involve Ken asking forgiveness, affirming his love for you and fidelity to you, and working with you to rebuild trust. Am I correct?"

"No, well, yes of course you are exactly correct. That is what I came in with, thought I wanted, but now I don't know." Again her jaw tightened some, her head lifted, she would not cry would not cry. "I'm not going to beg him to stay, not going to beg him to love me. So maybe this is the end, I don't know. Thank you, Doctor. I have to leave now."

Carole stood up abruptly and walked out of the office, fast, closing the door behind her. She left the building and started towards her car a half block away, but then stopped and entered a tiny park on the far corner from Dr. Ckeye's office. She sat on a bench under a tree, and looked at a cluster of daisies, sweet yellow with large black centers. After a few moments she saw Ken emerge, watched him walk away and around a corner. Carole sat a while and looked at the flowers. Round, pineapple-shaped bumblebees, black and yellow like the daisies they visited, worked flower to flower. The firm bench felt good. The sun was bright and warm, wind cool.

Chapter Eight

It was a week after the visit to Dr. Ckeye. Carole took Jamie to one of her friends who was having an evening birthday and slumber party. Carole ate alone, and then after cleaning up she called Trudy Miller, who lived across the street and down a few houses.

When Trudy had been married she and her husband Todd, both a few years older than Carole and Ken, got together every so often, more so in the summer, backyard cooking. Trudy had divorced three years ago, and went from a part-time to a full-time job. Now the women rarely saw each other, most often waving from a driveway upon arrival or departure. They would visit at one of the houses on the Fourth of July or New Year's day, but that was the extent of the friendship. Trudy would show up with a date. If the party was at Trudy's there would be her date, sitting in Todd's favorite chair.

Since they visited only twice a year, Carole lost track of the men, and couldn't always remember if she had met this one before, and if so last Fourth or New Years or two years ago. Ken never had those embarrassing problems; he talked baseball or upcoming Super Bowl, as appropriate. If the date didn't speak sports Ken moved on to someone who did.

"Hello, Trude, how are you? We never see each other. Would you like to come over for some dessert and coffee?"

There was a moment for voice recognition, and then Trudy said "You're getting a divorce."

"Oh no, the word is out already. Who told you?"

"Carole, no one told me. We haven't spoken much more than twice a year now for three years. Suddenly on a Thursday night you want coffee and girltalk? Not hardly. Divorce."

"I'm sorry, I should have been a better friend."

"Don't be silly. Our lives are too different -- all my old friends -- I have new friends. I see more of you than most of the married friends Todd and I used to have. It's just the way it goes. Now that we have something in common again maybe we'll -- sorry. Unnecessary dig. Why don't you come over here? I've got some cheesecake to die for."

Trudy welcomed Carole at the door and they went into the living room. The couch and curtains were different but complimenting patterns of warm earth tones, new since the divorce. They sat at opposite ends of the couch.

"So, what do you want right now, Carole? Sympathy, a shoulder, advice, what?"

"Advice. I really don't want to be foolish person."

"Advice. Fine. The first thing you do is find a good lawyer. Like mine, you might want to use her. Sophie Bertinski. And let me warn you about something. You need outsiders to help you - attorney, counselor, financial advisor. Listen to them, and just them. Getting advice from friends is not smart. In fact I can tell you from personal experience, it's really dumb. Everyone has some kind of axe to grind, or personal experience that doesn't fit your situation, or, well -- the point is find good advisors, listen to them, and politely ignore your friends' advice."

"Wait, I need to say something. Everything you say makes sense, and I want to hear it, but it is not certain that we are going to get divorced. Well, maybe almost certain, but I am trying to save it. Save the marriage. Save the sinking ship. Save the patient, dead on the operating table but the doctor won't quit."

"Yes, when to let go is always an interesting question.

This is one of those where you can get advice, but the decision is yours. Don't let anyone make it for you. Got someone to go to for professional help, a counselor or someone?"

"Yes, Ken and I went. What we accomplished is he got to say goodbye in front of a witness, not much more."

"Not sure if your marriage is really gone? But if it is, you should still go see someone, that counselor or another. Him or her?"

"Her, older woman, Dr. Ckeye, I liked her. I don't know, but probably I'll go back. At least maybe."

"More advice?"

"Please! I feel I should be taking notes."

"There are a lot of women's discussion groups in the area. I went to one like that before we split. Todd blamed some of our problems on the group. He was childish about me going to the meetings -- so threatened. 'Dykes, bitches and manhaters' he used to say. What a jerk! After we split I went back to one of them. Helped a lot. And I got some one-on-one counseling. The counseling was helpful, but I'm glad I spent time in a group. All I can tell you is to try a group or two, and if you are not comfortable with it or feel you need more direct help, go to a counselor. Or better, do both."

Trudy speared her cheesecake, then held the piece just above the plate as she talked. The cheesecake and coffee were served on a set of white china decorated with bold, purple tulips, the silverware a simple, modern pattern.

"Another thing. Take your time! Don't rush to decide, or sign, anything. Don't rush to end it, and if it is over, don't rush to court. One thing I learned from my group is how women can get screwed in divorce settlements because many are not used to thinking in dollars and cents. Of course, you do that for a living, so this probably doesn't apply to you. But there are some doozies. Like the wife who got an agreement to receive twelve hundred dollars a month for twenty years. Do you have any idea how little twelve hundred a month will be in twenty years? I don't know either, but some kind of cost of living number sure would have helped."

Carole sat quietly, listening, eating slowly. Trudy ate a forkful of cheesecake, then leaned back, waving her fork for emphasis. "So, who's the chick?"

"Well, he has a -- they were having sex, but he says she is not the reason. Has his own place, not with her. Rather embarrassing, Trudy. It appears that my husband has left me because he just stopped loving me, bored or something. Death of marriage by terminal boredom."

Trudy slouched lower in the couch. She hooked her toes into the heels of her shoes, kicking them off, then, put her feet on the low table in front of the couch. She sighed, arching her head back.

"Listen, Carole, there is some boredom in every situation. How long have you two been married? Twelve, thirteen?"

"Looks like we are going to make it into fourteen, anniversary soon, gone before fifteen."

"In these fourteen years you must have been bored once in a while." Trudy pushed down on the cushions with her elbows, dropped her feet to the floor and sat up.

"Bored? I don't know if that's the word. I thought we settled in the way we were meant to."

"And no Peggy Lee?"

Carole tilted her head slightly and smiled. "What?"

"Is that all there is? You never wondered about trying something or someone new?"

"I thought about it, sort of, but never really shaped it in my mind. It -- oh Trudy, it is so good to talk to you! I am sorry we fell away from each other. I want to be friends."

Trudy lowered her head, looking at her plate with most of the cheesecake gone. She started cleaning up, fussing, as a man would do with his pipe, not meeting Carole's gaze. She picked up the dishes and went to the kitchen. Carole felt her cheeks warm. She stood and walked through the dining room, her heels clicking softly on the polished wood floor. She stopped at the open door to the kitchen. Trudy was rinsing the dishes.

"I have the feeling I just said something quite wrong. What?"

Trudy turned off the water, then turned to face Carole. She reached out her right hand without looking and found the paper towel holder, pulled and tore and wiped her hands while talking. "We used to be friends. Then I got divorced, and the friendship died." Carole opened her mouth, but Trudy waved off the budding apology and continued talking. "It is not a question of the right thing to do, and I really don't want you to feel bad about what happened. We were together in a place in our lives. I guess the name of that place was marriage."

Trudy took a few steps toward Carole. Her voice was kind. "Then I left that place, or was thrown out. I got a real job and joined the wonderful world of the middle-aged divorced. Let me tell you, Carole, it stinks. Oh, I have some good times, and good laughs, but I sure would like to find me a reasonably worthwhile man and settle down. Come on, let's sit on the porch."

The screened-in porch was off the living room, and was fairly large, one of the nicest features of the house. There were several soft chairs along with a few wicker ones. There were tables and lamps, but the women left the porch in darkness, gazing out over the weedy garden to the hedge beyond, all faintly lit by the setting sun and a street light.

"The point is, if you do get divorced and we are again in the same place, the divorced place, then it would be fine to be friends. I mean that. But I want to be married. I am sick and tired of dating. I don't care if I never date again. If I find someone, or you do, then the one left behind will be dropped. That's just how things go."

"Sounds cold, Trudy. I suppose -- I'm thirsty. Do you want some water?" Carole said, rising.

"No thanks. Do you remember where the glasses are?"

"Yes, be right back."

Carole went to the kitchen, reached up to the right of the sink, and got one of the eight-ounce glasses with a frosted lace pattern. She ran the water a moment, then filled it and returned to the porch. She drank, then held the half-full glass in her lap, returning to her thought.

"I guess you're right but it, well, I said it, didn't I? Friendships switching on and off like that sounds so cold, so using."

In the gathering dark they did not have to look at each other, but sat almost parallel, looking at the shadows, like watching a fireplace.

"Carole, I have a friend who got divorced almost the same time I did. We went places together, dinners, cried on each other's shoulders, bar-hopped -- I'll have to tell you about that sometime -- dated the same men a few times, compared notes, like that. It was real nice for both of us. Maybe you and I will be like that. Maybe."

Trudy turned in her chair and faced Carole. They could barely see each other. "Four months ago she found someone. Now they are engaged, and of course I'm invited to the wedding. I'm trying not to be jealous, but I'm afraid I'm not doing so well. Oh, he's nothing special, but he'll do. Meanwhile she is crazy about him, giggling like a schoolgirl, screwing her brains out, and what do we have in common now? What can we share? Her happiness? My loneliness? My, don't I sound bitchy!"

They sat for long time, not speaking. Thinking. Their gazes again directed towards the lamp-lit garden and hedge beyond, Carole spoke softly. "I am overwhelmed by the change, all the questions, the things to be afraid of, to wonder about. I feel as though I've been hit by a truck and wasn't even near the highway. Thank you for this talk. And the advice. I hear you. Lots to think about, but suddenly I am so tired. I'm glad I can walk home, be afraid to drive." Both women rose and went towards the front door.

"I want to hear your bar-hopping and dating stories, but I can't begin to think of me doing that."

"Like I said, don't rush. Whatever happens, let it happen, don't push. Worry about dating when you're ready."

Carole stepped through the door into the comfortable night air, into the soft breeze. "I appreciate this. And the fine cheesecake, by the way. Maybe if dating happens I'll come back for more advice. Or invite you over, my cherry turnovers for your thoughts on dating."

"I'll tell you something I heard when I started out, and it is so true. Since you may be joining the sisterhood, I'll share it with you."

Carole smiled. "Why do I feel this is a good-news-bad-news line?"

"Smart lady. The good news is sometimes some singles find someone. The bad news, Carole, is that the single world abounds with dead ends."

"Abounds with dead ends. Hey, that cheered me up a lot! Well, I've got one for you. I lost a husband, but gained an extra twenty minutes in the morning, no bathroom polka." Carole hugged Trudy, they said goodnight. What she didn't say was that some mornings she used most of those twenty minutes putting ice on her eyelids so crying in the night wouldn't be detected by Jamie, by her co-workers.

Chapter Nine

A Saturday afternoon, no warning, Susan had a heart attack. She and Smokey were in the kitchen making apple pies, one for that night, the rest for the freezer or gifts. They worked as a team -- he preparing the dough and tending the oven, she mixing the ingredients and filling the shells. Suddenly she sat down on the floor, a handful of apple slices scattering. "Smokey, my chest hurts" and she looked at him, fear in her eyes. He grabbed the kitchen phone and dialed 911. While he held the phone and talked he put some towels down on the floor as a pillow and helped Susan lay back.

Smokey got two aspirins and gave them to her with some water, then sat by her until they heard the siren. From dialing 911 to the rescue wagon pulling up in front was only four minutes. Smokey opened the door and admitted two thin people, twenties or early thirties – a man with dark hair and mustache, a wiry woman with muscular arms. They were both carrying gray metal boxes.

Smokey didn't realize how scared he was until he tried to say "She's in the kitchen" and it came out part gasp, part squawk. He pointed and they went, he following and sitting down heavily on a kitchen chair.

The paramedics talked to Susan, calmly asking her to describe how she felt. The man went to get the wheeled stretcher, and they gently placed her on it. A few neighbors had gathered near the ambulance, or standing on the edges of their lawns. The children were curious and excited -- the grownups with somber faces and arms wrapped defensively around their bodies, or across the shoulders of loved ones, keeping the devil away.

The neighbors watched the four people emerge, the female paramedic backing up, guiding the stretcher down the stairs, reaching out and patting Susan's shoulder. Susan, oxygen mask strapped on, looked at her husband as they put her in the ambulance, locking eyes so tightly, he saying he would be right there.

The woman sat next to Susan's head and Smokey could see her leaning forward, talking to Susan. She was holding a blood pressure cuff, starting to put it on Susan's arm. The male paramedic shut the rear doors then turned to Smokey and said "Do you feel all right, Sir?"

"Yes, just a little dizzy. But go on ahead, go on. Mercy hospital?"

"Yes, Mercy. Sir, please don't drive yourself. Please get someone to take you." Pause. "Your wife will be fine."

Smokey nodded. The paramedic got behind the wheel and they pulled away. When he turned around Marge Polaren, a neighbor for many years, said "Come on Smokey, I'll drive you. Ready to go or do you need a few minutes?"

"Let me change my shirt -- we were baking pies" pointing to the flour on his shirt. He went in the house, turned off the oven, went into the bedroom and changed his shirt, grabbed his wallet, aware of his fear but keeping it away by keeping moving. As he came out of the house he found Marge waiting in the driveway, car's engine running.

Marge dropped Smokey off at the emergency room entrance. "I'm sorry, Smokey, I have to get back home, cousins coming from New York, expecting them in a half hour."

"My goodness Marge, don't worry, I really appreciate your taking me. I'm going to call my daughter as soon as I see what's up, and worst case there are always taxis. This is really great, thanks so much."

At the desk just inside the door Smokey gave the clerk the required personal and insurance information, then was told to have a seat, someone would be with him shortly. He sat for ten very slow minutes, then picked up a magazine for dog lovers and read an article about caring for the animals in the hottest summer months. When he looked at the clock again he saw only another three minutes had passed. Soon the desk clerk called his name. Standing up, he was met by a man in a white coat with a badge identifying him as Lincoln Phillips, M.D.

"Mr. Preater? I'm Doctor Phillips. Your wife is resting comfortably. We believe that she had a mild heart attack, but the cardiologist hasn't seen the EKG yet. So for now we are treating her for the symptoms and for the possible attack. Tell me, has she ever had heart trouble, or complained of chest pains or dizziness or numbing in her arms or fingers?"

"No, nothing like that. Some bad colds, pneumonia six or seven years ago, but aside from that nothing serious. When can I see her?"

"We are admitting her, make sure we know what we've got. Give us a little while and she'll be in her room. The desk clerk can tell you which one, probably know in a half hour. Please relax a bit if you can. She is stable, resting, and it appears to have been mild. Her vitals are fine. Why don't you have something to eat, call your family if you want to, and then see her. Really, I think she'll come through this with no problem."

Father called daughter.

"Hello?"

"Carole, honey, I'm at Mercy, emergency room. Your mother had a heart attack – well, they aren't totally sure, but it looks like. Doctor told me she's resting now. He said 'mild'-- that's what he thinks she had, a mild heart attack. I can see her in a little while."

"Dad, I'll be right there. In the emergency room?"

"Make it the cafeteria. I am suddenly starved -- nerves, I guess."

"OK, I'm on my way."

As soon as she hung up Carole realized that Ken would be bringing Jamie home soon from dinner. They usually were gone two hours, sometimes more if they went to a movie, but that wasn't planned for this evening. Carole wrote a hurried note and placed it on the table where family notes like this one were left, and keys, mail, and shopping lists were kept. She was glad Jamie had her own house key, but that prompted the thought that so did Ken. Carole drove faster than usual, not quite stopping at stop signs. Meanwhile, part of Carole's brain took that inappropriate moment to consider the fact that if they got divorced and she got the house all the locks would have to be changed. She wondered what that costs and who pays for it. "Stop that!" she said aloud, hushing the annoying, pragmatic voice.

Carole found her father finishing a ham and cheese croissant, cup of coffee. "Hi Dad."

"Hi honey. Glad you could come so quick. Want anything to eat?"

"No, unless we have to wait a while. I want to see Mom."

"She should have her room in a few minutes, maybe by now." He stood up, carried his empty paper cup and sandwich wrappings to the large beige trash bin with THANK YOU in bright orange above the opening. They walked into the hallway. "I thought you might have Jamie with you."

"She's with Ken. I left a note."

"Honey, I'm sorry about you and Ken. I should have called, but you know we seem to use your mother as our connector."

"Our message service. Don't worry about it. I was going to come over for a visit soon."

"Is he still out of the house?"

"Yes, and I think he is staying out. Gone. We don't have to do this now, talk about it. I'm sure we'll be spending some time together -- some in that cafeteria, no doubt."

They went to the ER desk clerk, who told them Susan was in 304. Walking in, they saw her hooked up to two monitors and an IV drip, her eyes closed, breathing softly. But at their first step into the room she opened her eyes and smiled, bathing both husband and daughter in relief. Smokey went to the bed and held Susan's hand.

"Hi, Sweet Sue" he whispered.

"Honey, did you turn the oven off?"

More reassurance. He smiled. "Yes dear, although there are some pies that won't make it to the dinner table."

"Hi, Mom."

"Hello precious. Now would you two please stop whispering? Normal voices won't hurt me -- it's my heart, not my ears."

A nurse stepped in. "Not too long, folks. A few more minutes, and then she should rest." They stayed the prescribed short visit, kissed her cheek and went into the hall, glancing back at her from the doorway. She seemed to have fallen instantly asleep. As they stood there, the nurse approached them.

"If you want to stay for an hour or so you can look in, and if she isn't asleep you may visit a bit more. But that will have to be all for today. You're welcome to wait, but if she's asleep I can't let you wake her. Here is the nurses' station number if you want an update" she said, handing Smokey a card. "And of course we'll call you if anything changes. But I don't want to alarm you. Her vitals are fine, positive indications. We'll take good care of her."

"Thank you, I'll stay" said Smokey. The nurse nodded, smiled warmly at both, and left. "I got dropped off by a neighbor, didn't drive. If you have to get home for Jamie I can take a cab."

"She can be alone, responsible young lady, although the refrigerator will suffer. You haven't seen her since before she went to camp, maybe five weeks now. Pops, wait till you see her. She is going from girl to young woman so fast it makes my head spin, and requiring a lot of fuel for the transformation. I left her a note, no problem. I'll be glad to stay and visit with you." They walked to the end of the hall to the Family Waiting Room and sat on a surprisingly comfortable couch. CNN was on a television facing them and they gave in, exchanging a few words now and then while glancing too often at the clock.

As Smokey and Carole were settling down in the waiting room, Ken was pulling into the driveway of his former residence to drop off Jamie. They had gone for dinner, this time to a wonderful Chinese restaurant, China Dynasty. They had Won Ton soup and shared Mu Shu Pork, both admiring the waitress's skill in assembling the roll-ups by using only spoons, no touching fingers. Their conversation, though, was a bit thin. Neither wanted to talk about the split or pending divorce, so they talked about movies and some of her friends and the fact that she would be learning to drive in less than four years. But they spent several long moments eating in silence.

When Jamie got out of the car with a "thanks, Dad" and a hug and a kiss, Ken waited until she had unlocked the door and gone in, giving him a quick wave. He put the car in reverse and had backed almost to the street when the front door flew open and Jamie came running out, a piece of paper in her hand, screaming for him to stop. She jumped in and said "Go to the hospital now!"

He read the note and for a tiny moment considered talking her out of it, considered asking her to wait until her mother came home, suggesting she could see grandma Susan tomorrow. But he knew that it would make Jamie angry, and he needed to keep as close as possible so they would stay friends through the stormy days to come. Stay friends through the divorce and afterward.

"OK, honey, go shut -- go lock the door."

Ken had not spoken to either of Carole's parents since the

split. As they drove to the hospital Ken tried to second-guess his wife. Had she told them only that there had been a bad argument? They must know he had moved out, but did she tell her parents about Sukie? What, how much, did they know? As they pulled into the four-story parking garage Ken guessed that his wife had not mentioned Sukie, or maybe said he was with Sukie but surely not about catching them soaping up. She wouldn't tell her mother that, would she? At best, this would be mildly embarrassing. At worst, Smokey would punch him in the nose, but what better place to be -- a hospital.

Jamie was out of the car and moving fast. Ken asked her to not run ahead, but when they came out of the walkway connecting the garage to the hospital Jamie sprinted to the information desk and had learned the room number by the time he got there.

"We haveto check in at the nurse's station on three first" she said, heading for the elevators.

The same nurse who had spoken to Smokey and Carole in Susan's room was now at the desk, and she told Ken and Jamie that they could visit in a half hour or so if Susan were awake, otherwise only look in from the doorway. She invited them to join the other family members in the waiting room.

This was what Ken was dreading most, so of course it came to pass -- waiting-room time with Carole and his father-in-law. Smokey stood up, said a reserved, uncomfortable "Hello, Ken" and shook his hand, then turned and gave a big, long hug to Jamie. She squeezed back, then went to her mother for another hug. Carole greeted Ken in a neutral tone, and he responded in like tone. Way lots he wanted out of that room. Jamie asked her grandfather what happened, and Ken was relieved that Smokey told the tale in some detail, using up several minutes.

Carole and her father had returned to the couch, and Ken sat in a chair along a wall at a right angle to the couch, Jamie sitting in a bean-bag chair in front of them. Smokey asked

Jamie about camp, and Ken was able to turn and focus on the television, CNN sports just starting. However, when the commercials came on he felt silly staring at them, so he turned back toward the others, from long habit catching his wife's eye. Carole looked at him, looked away. Jamie saw the looks, as did Smokey. What fun they all were having.

Ken picked up a magazine, as did Carole, while Jamie and her grandfather exchanged comments and watched the television. After a long fifteen minutes Carole said "It's been about an hour" and they all rose to check on Susan. Carole walked ahead with Jamie, and the men, hands in pockets, followed.

"I'm real sorry -- you and Carole. Hope you can fix things."

"Thanks, Smokey, I don't know what's going to happen, but don't worry about that now, please."

"Hard not to worry. Worry about Jamie, about Carole, about you. I like you a lot, Ken -- I'd hate to see you kids split up." Ken nodded acknowledgement.

Up ahead Carole and Jamie were talking to the nurse, who walked with them to Susan's doorway. Susan was awake, and smiled upon seeing them. "Please, only a few minutes, and no excitement" said the nurse, stepping aside. Jamie approached her grandmother with wide eyes and held her hand.

"Hi, baby, how was camp?"

As Jamie answered Smokey came in the room, followed by Ken. While Susan listened to Jamie she raised her eyes and looked right into her son-in-law's eyes, holding the stare. Ken had concluded that Smokey knew none of the details. The handshake and warm comments told him that. Not sure about Susan. Ken walked to the bed, leaned over and said "Hello, Susan."

"Ken. How are you?"

"I thought that was my line. Fine, Susan, just fine. And you? Ready to get up and leave this place?"

"Not tonight, I'm afraid, but soon." Her eyes stayed strong on his, far stronger than appeared possible from her pale color and the monitors and IV drip. Her eyes asked and challenged. Then Smokey stepped up and kissed her on the forehead, allowing Ken to break the grip of her gaze. Now he felt he could leave. Telling Susan he would be back he hugged Jamie, a brief, awkward hug, and walked out of the room. No good-bye or other acknowledgement towards Carole. He didn't even wait for the elevator, taking the steps for the three flights to the lobby. The movement felt good, let some of the tight springs uncoil. He still didn't know what Susan knew, couldn't even make a good guess. But he had committed to return, and he knew a stronger Susan without Carole or Jamie there would have a straight talk with him. Her eyes had promised that.

"Ernie, Mom's in the hospital. Heart attack, out of the blue, minor one. She seems to be doing fine, the doctors are pretty positive, she's awake and talking."

"When?"

"Sometime this morning. They were doing one of their pie bakes when it hit her. Dad says there's apples and flour all over the place."

"How is Dad?"

"Scared. They really need each other, you know?"

"I know. Is he staying with her?"

"No, they chased us all out so she could rest. He's probably mopping the kitchen floor right now and trying not to worry. I'll check on him in a little while."

"Me too. What a mess. Larry has a big meeting -- it's here in town but it starts Sunday, of all things. I don't think I can come until the next weekend."

"That's fine. There's nothing for us to do except worry, and you can do that long distance. Call Dad, that will mean a lot to him, and if you can come weekend after next that'll be great. Bring pictures of your crew -- that always makes Mom glad. And she really is doing OK. Breathing sounds normal, as I said, talking to us. Speaking of talking! Jamie was with Ken. I left her a note when I rushed to the hospital. Dad called me and I just flew out the door, so James sees the note and makes Ken bring her. He can't very well drop her off in front of the hospital --"

"Which one, I want to send flowers."

"Mercy."

"Go on, I want to hear the rest. Did he come up with her?"

"Sure, had to -- had to make sure she was safe. Not being sarcastic, I'm thankful he did that. Lots of people in and out of there and probably some of them nuts. So there he is, dutiful father with a 'help me I'm trapped' look on his face."

"Poor baby!"

"You should have seen the four of us sitting in the waiting room. Was it at all tense? Just a bit."

"How did Dad react? Does he know?"

"Neither of them knows about Sukie, and I hope they never do. So Dad did the man-to-man thing, 'hope you kids can work it out' speech."

Ernestine got a little teary-eyed. "Daddy. Hope he gets through this all right."

"Me too. He is scared."

"Did Mom see Ken?"

"Not only did she see him, but you know the look? The one we always got when we spent lunch money on candy?"

"Or put glue on the bottoms of --- what was her name?"

"Oh that's a while ago. Metrol or Mortill or something. Can't remember her first name either, but I do remember her trying to walk with glue on her soles. Well, Mom fixed him good with one of those looks. Heart attack or no, she skewered him. I think he thinks she knows all."

"What a moment. Too bad you couldn't take a picture right then, a family portrait."

"I'll call you tomorrow, give you an update. I don't know how long she is going to be there or if she is going to get a phone, probably will. How's Larry and your all-star crew?"

"Trading colds and sniffles, tissues when we can, sleeves and arms and pillows also in use. Very damp. Not a pretty sight, but the worst is over, and I should be clean and dry in two weeks. Larry is his steady self, keeps worrying about you. I think he would like the opportunity to give Ken a macho punch in the nose."

"OK by me."

"Jamie?"

"Concerned about her grandmother, little hard to read about Mommy and Daddy. Doesn't seem to be too upset, but I can't tell yet if that's a fake, or if she's highly mature and we bore her with our soap opera."

"I think I can come the weekend after, almost sure. As soon as I know I'll call. Maybe we can go have lunch at that greasy spoon Jamie loves."

"With extra ketchup."

"That's the one. Love you. Love Jamie, tell her."

"I will. Bye."

Chapter Ten

Obligations don't go away, responsibilities linger, the mind and conscience nag.

Ken knew he had to sit down with his mother-in-law -- sit down next to her while she lay in the hospital and be honest, be a man about it. He was dumping her daughter, and he should say it, straight up.

As he thought about it, readied himself for the phone call and the meeting, he became aware of how much he cared for Susan -- really loved her. And this was the end. He had no doubt this was likely the last close conversation he would have with her for a long time, maybe forever. Perhaps at Jamie's wedding, or the birth of her first child. If he should live so long. If Susan should live so long. Ken shook his head, guilty and upset that the thought had even formed.

Ken felt he had to have this conversation. He and Smokey got along well enough, but without nearly so close, so strong a bond as he had with Susan. And he did not want to try to talk to her at home, because Smokey and friends and neighbors would be there. No, he needed to be alone with her to answer the questions that had been in her eyes the day she had the heart attack. Worried that she would soon be released, he waited only two days and then called to check on her status. Learning that she was listed in good condition, he got her room telephone number and called.

"Hello, Susan. Is this a good time?"

"Well, I was about to trip the light fantastic, but for you I'll wait a moment. Nurse, ask the band to hold that tune."

"I was going to ask how you're feeling, but it sounds like you are just fine."

"Well, I'm going to be around for a while. That's what the doctors tell me. A day or two more and I can go home, let Smokey fuss and spoil me."

"I want to talk to you. I guess I need to talk to Smokey too, but I want a few moments alone with you. May I?"

"Certainly. Smokey comes every morning about ten. I am awake about six or six thirty, breakfast is at seven. Any time after seven-thirty is fine."

"Seven-thirty. See you then."

He arrived to find her not in her bed, but sitting in the yellow leather chair next to it. Susan was wearing fuzzy yellow slippers, almost the same color as the chair, white pajamas covered with a pattern of multi-colored little cats and dogs, and a white hospital gown serving as a light robe. He awkwardly bent down and kissed her cheek. "Give me a hand, Ken. I need to walk. Let's walk to the elevator, I'll show you the sights."

Ken helped her stand, and holding his arm they walked slowly towards the elevator. The hall was clean and bright. At the far end an elderly man guided an enormous wet mop back and forth over the floor. Although her step was a bit slower than usual, Susan stood straight and walked comfortably, her arm through his but not leaning on him. When they got to the elevator she reached out and pushed the UP button.

"Where are we going?"

"A nice place to talk."

The nice place was the roof patio, with chairs and tables, benches, and potted flowers, mostly petunias of blue, purple, salmon, and white. They started towards a bench, but Susan said "No, two chairs. I want to look you right in the eye." The heart attack had weakened her physical self, not her spirit.

They sat.

"You moved out, Ken. I can't believe it. I can't believe you're still out, and I'm certainly concerned about everything, everybody, especially Jamie. Carole has told me almost nothing, and I'll respect your privacy, too, but you said you wanted to talk to me. I was glad to hear that. So?" She opened her hands in a waiting gesture.

Susan did not know about Sukie. As Ken realized that he also knew he should have guessed that at once; if Susan had known she wouldn't have received him as she had, pleasantly though not very warmly. "I need to tell you two things" he said.

Susan drew back, her posture stiffening, her hands folded tightly in her lap. "You aren't going to like the first, but please let me say both."

"And I need to hold your arm to get back to the room, so I guess I have to hear it all." Her voice was soft, firm, her face solemn.

"I'm not going back. It's over, and it is all my doing. My decision. I haven't wanted to be married for some time. This is coming out pretty disjointed, sorry. I actually rehearsed some, Susan, but I'm not doing a very good job of it." He rubbed his face in the familiar gesture. Susan sat quite still, leaning back against the chair, face set, hands still folded. Her eyes were strong, digging into his.

"I was in love with your daughter, and now I'm not. I wanted to be married, and now I don't. It's that simple, and that incredibly complicated."

"Is there another?"

"I am not leaving Carole for anyone else, no, not that at all" he side-stepped. "I don't want to be married. It isn't anything about Carole, and please believe I'm not just saying that. It is me, my head. I apologize for hurting Carole, and you and Smokey and Ernestine and Larry. And I have apologized, and sure will again, to Jamie for breaking up our home. I am going to work real hard at being as good a father as I can after the divorce. I want so much for Jamie to get through this without any---without it making growing up any more difficult than it already is. But Susan, I can't apologize for falling out of love. I didn't ask for it, certainly didn't plan on it."

Susan paused, her strong eyes still searching. "And the second item?"

"You have been a great friend, a wonderful mother-in-law. We won't be together much now, and I will miss you. I wanted you to know that I will miss you."

"So that's it? I hear the words, and don't for a minute doubt you are sincere, but as you said, you aren't apologizing, are you Ken? You are explaining."

"Yes."

"And so you walk away. Too bad, you just don't love the girl anymore, and so off you go. I'm not going to raise my voice or blood pressure, but I'm not satisfied." She paused, looked away, took a deep breath and let it out slowly. Then Susan turned back to him and continued in the same firm, calm voice.

"I don't dislike you, Ken, but I intensely dislike what you are saying. Do you think your responsibility to Carole, to Jamie, is only money? You made promises, vows, have been a husband and father for over thirteen years, and now, what, you want to leave with no more explanation than that your pilot light has gone out?" Again Susan paused, rested, looked away and back.

"Susan, I expected you to be upset and I'll take the lecture, but I don't think you should be doing this now. I'll bet the doctors wouldn't approve of this conversation, probably not the best therapy."

"Don't you go ducking out, Kenneth. You asked for this little chat, and we are chatting. Besides, I'm almost done. I never thought I would say this to you, but you aren't being adult about this. You're making a mess and walking away, as if admitting to making the mess were sufficient. What's it that the kids say? 'My bad?' So you say 'My bad' to your wife and daughter, and to me and the family, and that's supposed to suffice? Don't you have a responsibility to try to save your marriage, honor your vows? How about counseling, therapy? How about going away with your wife for a while?"

"You know, I remember when you two decided to get married. Ken, you were so in love you couldn't see straight. I was worried when you went out driving with her because you couldn't keep your eyes off her. I thought you'd run into a telephone pole staring at Carole. Why don't you take a week, go someplace with her and talk and work at trying to find again that reason you fell for her. It wasn't so long ago, you know, and neither of you has changed that much that I can see. And you know what?" Susan leaned toward him. Their noses were six inches apart.

"My daughter, who is good looking, smart, funny, and a lot of other things such as the mother of your child, loves you. *Loves* you. Are you sure you want to give that up? Might be, well, there is no other word is there? Might be real stupid of you to give her up."

Not sure how to answer, he just agreed. "Yes, it might be stupid. I know. I can't make any promises to you." Wrong word. Promises. They both knew.

He didn't say no, but that is what he meant. Susan nodded her head several times, small short nods for understanding, not acceptance. Her eyes dropped from his, and the fire faded. She suddenly looked smaller, older, very tired.

"Are you all right? Do you want me to call a nurse?"

She raised her eyes again, now beginning to tear. "You have broken my heart, Kenneth Tagee. First a heart attack, and now a broken heart. A lot for a woman of a certain age to bear. Please help me back to my room."

They walked back in silence, Susan again holding his arm, leaning a bit more on him for support. In the room she took off her slippers and robe, and he offered his hand to help her into bed.

"I hope I did the right thing by coming to see you today. I

sure didn't want to stress you."

"You did the right thing. I wanted to know what was going on -- have wanted to know since Carole told me you moved out. Thank you for coming, Ken." She closed her eyes.

Ken stood there a moment, then said "Get well soon, Susan. And please never hesitate to call me if you or Smokey need help. I mean that. I can be there for you."

Eyes still closed, Susan nodded one small nod. Ken turned and quietly left the room.

Susan continued to improve and was released two days later. The next weekend Ernestine came up, arriving late Friday night. Her old bedroom had been turned into Susan's sewing room, Carole's into an office and storage area, but a single bed in Ernestine's and a bunk bed in Carole's had stayed, useful for family visits. Since Jamie was with Ken, the girls came home for the weekend.

In a turn of life's wheel as old as civilization the children took care of the parents, cooking and serving and cleaning. Smokey had no chores for those two days. He tried to object, but his daughters insisted he take the time to sit with Susan and rest, because he would have the burden again Monday morning.

Carole and Ernestine gave the whole house a good cleaning, working side by side much of the time, talking constantly, conversation yielding only to the vacuum cleaner. Susan was required to walk each day, so she took two short walks both Saturday and Sunday, the other three walking with or behind the patient. Neighbors came out of their homes and greeted Susan. "Thank goodness you're home, how are you feeling?" "Please let me know if you need anything, anything at all." "How nice to have your girls home again."

It was a great time for all four. They shared meals, got out the family albums and boxes of pictures yet to be put in albums. They remembered events and told stories, most already known but comforting to hear again. Carole and Ernestine talked about their children, their latest adventures, how fast they were growing. They talked about Larry. No mention of Ken.

Sunday afternoon the house was quiet. Carole slipped off her shoes and walked as gently as possible down the hall to her parent's bedroom, where she stopped at their open door. The sun streamed in the big bedroom windows. Susan was in bed, dressed in slacks and a tee shirt, a light comforter pulled up to her waist. She was deeply asleep. Smokey sat in a big, overstuffed chair that usually was against a wall but he had moved closer to the bed. He had been watching her sleep and had fallen under himself, his head back, snoring softly. To Carole it seemed the room shimmered and glowed from their love. She heard Ernestine approaching but didn't take her eyes off their parents, then Ernestine joined her at the doorway and put an arm around her waist. They stood and memorized the sight, tried as hard as they could to burn it into their memories.

Chapter Eleven

So much of what was happening seemed to Carole as if it were happening to someone else, as if she were watching a woman she knew go through the phases of divorce, the task-by-task end of a marriage. This feeling was fading, reality becoming clearer, more accepted if not acceptable.

One step was becoming public about the situation. When Carole told the people she worked with, she just made a brief statement that Ken had moved out and they were trying to deal with some personal problems. Little was said after that. She only lost it at work one time, months after the break-up, already working towards the divorce. And it was such a dumb thing. Carole had been pushing back and pushing back the pain, sealing it up, covering it with tons of concrete so she could get on with her life. Working on the files, pulling some old ones and sorting them for trash or storage, and there was last year's Valentine's Day card, unexplainably in a file of accounting records. She should have pitched it, but could not stop herself reading his words "Thank you for being my everything. I love you so." It would have been nice to laugh like Bette Davis and pitch it, but it just caught her so wrong, tired and in pain and popping up unexpected like that. She gasped and cried out and ran to the ladies, went in a stall and sat down and cried and cried. When she emerged she saw people carefully not looking at her, and when she got to her desk noticed the card was gone. Carole never found out who got rid of it, never asked, wasn't told. She resolved never to break down at work again.

Going to a mediator was another step towards divorce. The county court requires that any couple filing for divorce that has a child must go through mediation of the parenting agreement. A list of mediators who have been approved by the court, and their credentials, are presented to each couple. The final choice is up to the couple and is made for many reasons -- because one of the attorneys recommended a specific mediator, or by recommendation from a friend, or because they like the mediator's credentials or simply because one party insists it has to be a man or a woman.

By now Carole and Ken had attorneys. Norman Jones was known and respected by both attorneys and was quickly chosen. He was a professor of sociology who became interested in mediation after reading several articles on the subject. He took a short course, began mediating disputes between students on a voluntary basis, then took more training, got an office and began mediating for a fee. At first it was very occasional, not paying much more than his office rent and expenses, but as his reputation grew he took more training, began to advertise, and eventually took early retirement to become a full-time mediator.

Carole and Ken arrived separately, but at almost the same moment, parking near each other. He had a thick portfolio under one arm, she only a newly-purchased notepad in her purse. Carole glanced at the portfolio, frowned slightly but said nothing. He proceeded her to the door, but the portfolio was under his right arm and he couldn't easily reach across his body to open the door with his left hand. Carole stepped around him and opened the door, holding it for him, he murmuring thanks.

Norman Jones came out of his office as they walked into the small waiting room, greeting them and showing them to the mediation room. It was ten by sixteen feet, with indirect lighting glancing off walls painted a soft blue, an eggshell ceiling. All around the room, about five and a half feet from the floor, was a six-inch strip of corkboard. The dark wood conference table held six comfortable armchairs, two on each long side. At the far end from the door, behind the chair at that end of the table, stood two easels. On the table, and on small side tables, were tablets, pencils, small calculators, pushpins for the corkboard, small tissue boxes.

The mediator had placed a tablet and several pencils in front of two chairs, one on each long side, his place clearly between the easels. A moment of hesitation, and then Carole walked around the table to one chair, Ken taking the one opposite.

"Thank you for coming. As you know, my name is Norman Jones. Please call me Norm. May I call you Carole?"

"Yes.

"And you prefer --"

"Ken's fine."

"Thank you. I understand you have decided to divorce and would like me to mediate a parenting agreement for your daughter, Jamie. If you wish, I can mediate other aspects of your divorce, such as your financial agreement, but that does not have to be decided now.

You both have attorneys. I encourage you to check with your attorney as often as you feel necessary. We likely can reach a parenting agreement in two sessions, plus a little homework on your part. If you want to speak to your attorney before and between each session, or wait until there is a final agreement and speak to your attorney before you sign, it's up to you. As often as you feel is necessary, whatever you need to be comfortable."

"Is that signed agreement a legal document?" Ken asked.

"I am not an attorney and cannot give legal advice. In fact, I was going to say that soon, it is on my check list," he said, indicating the sheet under his right hand.

"Sorry."

"Not at all. It's an important question, and you may want to ask your attorney. Let me say, however, that while I cannot say if it is a legal document I encourage people never to sign something they wouldn't want introduced in court."

He paused a moment, looking at both in turn, they looking back at him. "This is a contract that spells out what my services are, and what you agree to do in attempting to reach a mediated agreement. I am going to read it word for word. Please feel free to stop me if you don't understand something."

Norm withdrew three identical pages from a folder, handing one each to Carole and Ken. He then read the page, pausing when he came to the line that said "The fee of $150.00 (one hundred fifty dollars) per hour will be paid _____ % by _________ and _____ % by _________"

"Have you decided this?"

"I assumed we would split it" Carole said to Norm. She turned towards Ken who shrugged and said "Sure."

"So what goes in these blanks is fifty percent by Carole Tagee and fifty percent by Kenneth Tagee, correct?" he said, pen poised above the paper. They both answered by nodding. Norm filled in the blanks, and continued reading. The agreement called for full disclosure of assets and a promise not to move or hide any assets, nor to make expenditures other than normal, anticipated household expenses until the divorce is final. Carole and Ken agreed, both thinking private money thoughts.

When Norm finished reading he asked if they had any questions, and when they did not he asked them to sign, promising a copy for each before they left.

"This first session consists of two parts. First, I want to talk about what present arrangements you have for your daughter, then we can start building the permanent agreement. Jamie is – twelve?"

"Thirteen next week" said Carole. "She was born thirty days before our first anniversary." She looked at Ken, but he gave her profile, looking intently at the mediator.

"The second part will be homework, things to think about before our next session. We may be able to finish an agreement about care for Jamie, and your parenting agreement, in that session. Am I correct that you are not asking me to mediate your financial settlement -- that is, the division of your marital assets?

"Not at this time, the parenting agreement was the only part the court required us to mediate" said Carole.

"But we might. Let's see how this goes."

"Fine Ken, and Carole, let's work out the parenting agreement and then, if you decide so at a later date, I would be pleased to help you with your financial settlement. OK, part one. How are things working now? What are you doing regarding Jamie's needs, her care, housing?"

"Well, Jamie is living with me."

"And that is the family home?" Norm said, beginning to write on a tablet.

"Yes."

"Let me say to both of you that I am going to be asking what seem like unnecessary questions -- questions where the answers would appear to be obvious. The reason I will be doing that is because I don't want to assume anything. Here comes the first. Ken, you have moved out?"

"Yes. Jamie is with Carole, I get to see her whenever I want. Carole has been great about that." He turned towards her. "You have been great about that. Thank you."

She nodded. "I'm not going to play games with Jamie. This isn't about Jamie. This is about you and me. And Sukie. I don't want Jamie visiting you, spending the night, while you're with her."

"I'm not with her. Can we do what we came here to do?"

Norm gently, firmly intervened. "It sounds as if you are cooperating about Jamie spending time with both parents. I applaud you, I mean that. I hear some terrible stories in this room about people using their kids, time with their kids, as a trading card, a chess piece. You aren't doing that. Great."

"What do we need to settle now?" Ken said with a touch of impatience.

One of Norman Jones's strengths is his ability be neutral, to maintain neutral language and posture. His answer showed no reaction to Ken's tone. "Carole expressed concerns about Jamie being with you and" he glanced quickly at his notes "Sukie. You responded that you aren't with her. Perhaps some clarification is needed."

"I am not living with Sukie. She has visited me in my apartment. I would never have Jamie and her at my place at the same time."

"Does that respond to your concern, Carole?" When she nodded, he continued. "What have you worked out about expenses, clothing and food? And shelter. Is there a mortgage?"

"Yes. Carole and I each have our own checking accounts and also a household account. I've put my half into the account since -- since I moved out."

"Nothing for utilities, or for Jamie."

"I've had expenses."

"A result of your wandering penis."

"Oh shit, Carole!"

Again the neutral, firm voice of Norman Jones. "These are exactly the things that are best for mediation. Sharing time, sharing expenses. Carole, it sounds like there are some issues about expenses that you may want to address at this session. I know you haven't asked for mediation of all assets and liabilities, you may or may not want my help with those, but money concerns when it comes to Jamie, well, they are on the table now."

"Yes. I have been paying all the utilities. It is true that Ken put money in for the mortgage, but that's all. Gas, electricity? And like I said, clothing and food."

"If you both approve, all those will be part of the final mediated agreement. Would one of you like to propose something for the interim?"

They sat for a moment. Carole picked up her pencil and began writing numbers on the pad, multiplying, adding. Ken watched her a moment and began his own calculations.

"Calculators if you need them" Norm said, gesturing. Neither took him up on the offer. He sat back and waited.

"You have been out of the house for six weeks. How about eighty a week, not counting the mortgage, which we can split for now?"

"I would have guessed more. You sure?"

"Sure."

"I'll send you a check for nine weeks, through the end of the month, OK?"

"Are you two going to be so agreeable about everything? I feel like the world's best mediator."

Husband and wife said, together, "Don't count on it." Embarrassed by the intimacy, they jotted on their papers, not looking at each other.

"We're just about finished. I do want to give you copies of the agreement you signed, take just a minute. While I make them, please look at these."

He handed them a small stack of papers. They included a two-sided page that listed national, religious, and ethnic holidays. Other pages referenced food, clothing, housing, health insurance, doctor and dentist costs beyond insurance, health care items such as over-the counter medicines, social and summer camp expenses and other items regarding the expenditures that come with caring for children. One page labeled "School year" and another labeled "Summer" were blank except for a grid of five weeks, Sunday through Saturday.

When Norm returned he handed them each a copy, and sitting again put the original in a file. "These are sketch pages, and I encourage you to make copies, keep a clean original. Fill them in as best you can. Propose an agreement. As an example, one of you may feel you want Jamie with you every Fourth of July, the other every Memorial Day. Or, you may want to alternate major holidays. Do you celebrate any religious holidays?"

"Christmas and Easter, pretty much. Some church, that's usually just Carole and Jamie. I don't go all that often but always the big two, a C and E Christian."

"A little more church might have been good for you."

Ken ignored her. Norm continued. "For major holidays, religious holidays some families alternate, year on – year off. Or even share a day, mornings and evenings. Lots of options. Think about what you would like to do about the school year and summer vacations. And think about the expenses listed here, and any the form may have missed. As I've said, it is up to you how much of your financial situation you want to mediate, beyond the care-of-Jamie items. These pages give you guidelines should you want to mediate other financial questions."

He handed them each one more form. "Your attorneys may have given you this, but I want to also. This is the standard visitation rule, the fallback position of the court. If you cannot reach a mediated agreement the court will impose it on you. It is fair and reasonable, but it is also a formula, not designed by you. The best thing about mediation is that you" -- as he said "you" he looked directly at each in turn -- "own the process, design the agreement. It is yours, the Ken Carole Jamie agreement, not the generic agreement. Please don't lose sight of that should there be sticking points."

They nodded, both deep in thought, already mentally sketching schedules. After agreeing to meet in two weeks at the same time both got up, ready to leave. Ken put the page from his tablet in his otherwise unused portfolio, shook Norm's hand, confirmed the next appointment and left. Carole shook his hand, turned and followed Ken out of the room. This time he held the door for her, she murmuring thanks. They spoke no more as they walked down the building's sidewalk to the end, where they parted, each to their own cars.

Chapter Twelve

Ever in the mood for Italian food, Carole had lunch at one of her favorite places -- a neighborhood, family-owned spaghetti house. Although she had been there many times, a picture she had paid little notice to before caught her attention -- a print of an oil painting of Venice. A tall, lean gondolier worked his pole, pushing his vessel through a canal, a stone bridge curving above his shoulders. In front of him was seated a young couple holding hands. It had never before struck Carole that the young woman was gazing lovingly at her partner, while the young man sat sideways to her, as if better to present a square jaw for her adoration. "Painted by a man, no doubt" thought Carole. Next to the painting was a bulletin board with lost dogs, kittens for free, an estate sale, babysitter available, female roommate wanted and similar notices. One notice read:

LONELY? WORRIED? CONFUSED?
WOMEN'S CIRCLE, A SUPPORT GROUP
HELPING OTHERS - OTHERS HELPING YOU
SUNDAYS, 7:00 p.m. to 9:00 p.m.
SHALOM VILLAGE COUNSELING CENTER
COLLEGE AVENUE AT BRIDGE STREET

Carole wondered if, like the jawline in the gondola, men/

women pictures and writing would now come to her attention differently than in the past. She had never noticed the poster before, although from its multiple pinholes it appeared to have been on the bulletin board for a while, moved several times. Carole remembered Trudy mentioning the good such groups can do. She opened her purse, took out her appointment book, and copied the information.

What does one wear to a women's support group meeting? Carole was reminded of the old psychiatrist joke about appointments -- come early and you're anxious, come on time and you're compulsive, come late and you're hostile. She sat on the edge of her bed, dressed in bra and pantyhose, and felt caught in a similar trap. No makeup means you are angry at or not interested in men? No makeup means you are secure in your selfhood? Wearing makeup means being a victim? Being fashionable? Being sexy? Slacks? Sweater? What does it say about your sense of identity? Maybe nothing. Maybe nothing at all, just Carole being nervous about new people, a new situation. In the end she settled on a simple skirt and blouse and her usual light blush and lipstick.

Carole arrived early, wanting to make sure she had time to find the room and sign in or do whatever new members do. The meeting was held in a small conference room, twenty or so folding chairs with brown cushions and metal backs gathered in a circle. As she walked in she was greeted by a short woman in loose, comfortable clothes who spoke in a warm, sincere voice.

"Welcome, I'm Judy Pagges, the moderator" she said, shaking Carole's hand.

"Hello. Carole Tagee. Do I sign in somewhere?"

"No signing in. I count heads each time, but no list." Judy motioned toward a table with two slightly battered coffee urns and a smaller pot. "Regular, decaf, water for tea."

"Thank you." Carole walked to the table and made herself a cup of tea in a coated paper cup, adding a half packet of sugar. Several women introduced themselves, first names only, and welcomed her. Carole tried to remember names but then settled on remembering Judy's. Turning towards the circle of chairs, she noticed a recorder sitting on a small stool in the middle of the floor, a short black cord connected to a brown extension cord stretching to the wall. Coming out of the other end of the recorder was a device that sent out four cords to four microphones pointed outward, four compass points, at the chairs.

Judy walked up to Carole. "I usually explain things for new members when the group starts, but since you're our only one tonight, let me tell you quickly. I am working on my master's degree and leading a counseling session is a requirement. My instructor listens to the tapes with me and comments on the sessions, my techniques as a moderator, then the tapes are erased. I'm really lucky to have him as a mentor, doctor Frank L. Roberts, a psychiatrist with enormous experience.

"How much longer will the sessions last, when are you done?"

"Another six weeks, but I have been talking to the director about keeping them going, about their paying me to run the sessions on a permanent basis. It looks like they are going to do it, in fact we may start another group sometime during the week, Tuesday or Wednesday nights."

At about five past seven the group sat down. There were seventeen, the youngest about twenty-five, the oldest sixty-five or seventy.

"My name is Judy. Welcome. We have a new member, Carole," Judy said, nodding towards her. "Please remember to say your name when you talk the first time. Now, any unfinished business from last time? Any good news to share? Or urgent hassles?" Judy sat straight up in her chair, her hands flat, relaxed on her thighs. She would lift a hand to gesture and then return it to its resting place.

A pause. "No? Well, who'd like to start?"

"Hi, Jennifer here. So I've been coming a while, really

like the talk, the sharing. Really like it. So last time we were talking about cooking, about who cooks, who shops, all that stuff. Got me thinking about when me and my ex first got into it. We was living together, gonna marry when the money was better. Meanwhile I'm doing all the real cooking, he's bringing home food, never fixing it. So I lean on him, tell him 'A pizza and a six-pack just don't get it.' Shoulda seen that as big red flag, shoulda."

Jennifer's sharing was met with various comments about men cooking in restaurants but not at home, a few saying their man can cook but is, or was, a lot of trouble.

"I'm Rhonda. Me and my sister was talking about starting a child care service, maybe in her house to start. Anybody know about that business?"

"I know there aren't enough good ones."

"Or any cheap ones!"

"Names, please" said Judy.

"Sorry. My name is Gloria," said the second woman. She was wearing a brown and cream checked shapeless top, brown slacks with some threads pulled, white socks and scuffed white sneakers. "When you ain't makin' but seven thirty-five an hour you can't pay full price, don't get your kids in some charity place there ain't no way. For a while the place I take my baby was full up, I had used up my turn and others came first, only fair I know, but I thought I'd have to quit my job till they had some openings."

"It sounds like there is a need for your service, Rhonda," said Judy, others nodding their heads and offering comments of agreement. "How far along are you in the planning?"

"Well, we sat down and tried to figure out the money, you know, like a family budget. I'm real good at making a dollar stretch, my husband says I make a buck sing like a bird. So I sat down with Mary, that's my sister, Mary, an' we worked it around to see what we needed to make out, to make money, what we had to charge. Mary, she had a good idea, what we did is figure close as we could what it would cost to run it, just the costs, you know? Nothing in our pockets. So if we had, took care of say eight kids, we divided our costs by eight and that was our base, our got-to-have for each child we're watching. So then if we wanted to pay ourselves it would be on top of that. We're thinking start at her place, eight kids to start, the two of us. Got to have a license for that many kids, and someday a bigger place, some help, be able to charge more if we hire a real teacher. Someday. Got to start somewhere, so we're thinkin' start small and see how it goes, learn the business then try to make it grow."

The discussion continued -- some advice on agencies and government offices to consult and encouragement was offered to Rhonda. The conversation veered off into child raising questions, concerns about discipline and religious upbringing. The members offered advice, ideas, comments, experiences to each other. Judy guided gently, making sure a question was addressed if the conversation changed direction before there was an answer, making sure the more vocal ones didn't capture too much of the time. Carole realized she hadn't spoken, but looking around the room realized that four or five others hadn't spoken either.

When the session ended Carole walked up to Judy. "I didn't intend not to contribute, but I got so involved listening that it never occurred to me to say something. I do want to come back, I really enjoyed it, and I'll pitch in next time."

"Please come back, but don't feel pressed to contribute. This is for the members, for people to get what they need out of it. A few have been coming for weeks and said almost nothing. If the room goes quiet I will try to bring them in, 'How do you feel about that' or a similar question, but the theory, the model we are using is that some use the circle for healing, some for information to grow, to move on or up as Rhonda did tonight, some for the companionship. If a woman wants to think of us as almost family, if she gets comfort from hearing us talk as though we were all around the family dinner table, I'm not going to make her feel uncomfortable, maybe drive her away by insisting she talk each time. I believe, and doctor Roberts believes, that people who come and sit and listen are getting at least part of what they need, and that is a good thing. Sometimes it's a delicate balance, and we don't want to upset them."

"Interesting. If you don't mind, one more question."

"No, that's fine."

"More of an observation, really. My ignorance, or maybe prejudice. I thought we would be talking more about men than we did."

Judy smiled. "And indeed we do. I let the group go its way, take its head. I keep it going, clarify, draw people out as I said, but I never set the agenda, except to make sure that any unfinished business from the last session is taken care of. Sometimes there is a hot subject and we run out of time, so I like to start there next session. But as for men, if you come to these on a regular basis you will find we spend a lot of time talking about men. Ex-husbands, boyfriends, ex-husbands punching boyfriends, ex-husbands going fishing with boyfriends, ex-husbands making passes at boyfriends. And money. And sex. And divorce. Arguing over kids. In-laws, lots of in-laws discussions. And self-esteem, self-image, anger, pride, victory and defeat. Or defeat and victory, sounds better."

"Sounds like it's always interesting."

"Always, and some people get a lot of help. I'm glad you've joined us. Please come back."

"Thank you. Goodnight."

Chapter Thirteen

"Hey, Carole. It's Rozanne Berg. How have you been?"

"Well just fine, Rosie. Good to hear from you. And you?"

"As always. And better."

"Let me guess. The book club."

"Yes indeed! Time to spark those synapses, offer opinions, think great thoughts. We haven't reviewed a book in six months, and our minds are all the worse for it. I think I can get six or seven, maybe eight. Got to work the old phone list."

"I could be tempted. What are we reading?"

"Yet undecided. I found three books, haven't read them but have two reviews for each. We meet at my house, I feed you such calories you shouldn't eat again for a week, we read the reviews, we vote. Intellectual democracy in action."

"Wednesday night? As usual?"

"Not this one, week from. Can you come?"

"I won't have dessert from now till then. Seven?"

"Seven. Great. See you then."

The fates stirred their wicked brew, howled, rolled and soared. Carole should have seen it coming, heard alarm bells in her head. None. Oblivious to the obvious she went to the meeting, light of heart and step. Of course Jamie had a minor emergency, cut a finger in the kitchen, so Carole was the last to arrive. One seat left. On a love seat. Next to Sukie Powers.

A moment of recognition, then they avoided each other's

eyes, polite smiles fixed. Carole sat carefully, hugging her side of the love seat.

Rozanne said "That's everyone, we're all here. A few new members, welcome welcome. Can we just quickly go around the room and say our names?"

At her turn Carole considered saying "Mrs. Kenneth Tagee" but of course didn't. Rozzane said "Great, thanks. The agenda. First a little work, then a little nosh. That's Yiddish for calories. I put the reviews on one page, made some copies. Everyone please share" she said, passing them out.

Two people on a love seat would naturally share, right? Carole, with as little body-english as possible, indicated Sukie should go first. While Sukie read, Carole scanned the room, peeking out from under her eyebrows looking for telltale signs of titillation or embarrassment or glee. None. No sideways glances or knowing looks. They couldn't all be such fine actors. Somehow Ken and Sukie had been secretive about his nocturnal and other-hours' visits. Somehow they had avoided anyone knowing. Well, good. No, great. Thanks, Ken and Sukie. How quaint. Rake and slut, but at least discreet.

When she had first seen Sukie and sat next to her, Carole felt an unpleasant combination of queasy, angry, embarrassed, topped off with an adrenaline rush. With the realization that no one knew her relationship via Ken to her couch partner, Carole began to relax, and the humor of the situation became prominent. She could sit there and be cool. If Sukie could do it then Carole sure could too.

The books Rozanne had chosen were all documentaries. One dealt with the immigration of people from Eastern Europe in the thirty years preceding World War I. The second was about the life and times of artists in France, primarily Paris, in the years between the World Wars when art flourished there. The third was about American pioneers, a hard but factual look -- not the Hollywood version but the truth about childbirth, cooking, life and death during the slow trek west. The third was viewed as too somber, the second too much fun, so immigration won.

A brief debate took place as to whether this book merited three weeks or four weeks before the review and discussion meeting, but since there had not been one for so long people were eager to get going again. Three weeks was the choice. Two of the guests offered to have the event at their houses, and it was decided they would decide, or flip a coin, while refreshments were served. Coffee, tea, many fine candies, mostly chocolate, two pecan-encrusted coffee cakes, and fresh fruit for those refraining from caloric indulgences.

Although they all lived in the same general area, Carole realized she had not seen several of the women since the last book club, and she enjoyed talking with them. Rozanne had been able to find six women to accept her invitation, and they split into two groups of three for the desserts and conversation. Rozanne, the perfect hostess, was pleased to see them thus, and she moved back and forth between them, offering comments and refills. Carole was in one cluster, Sukie in the other.

By that magic unspoken signal, all knew when it was time to leave. The first to thank Rozanne and make her exit was Sukie. Carole fantasized calling after her "Sorry you have to rush off. Hot date?" No such antagonism, let sleeping dogs lay. Lie. Lay and lie. She realized that Rozanne was asking her a question. "I'm sorry, Rosie, lost in a fog. Please try again."

"I'm asking several of the girls if they would scout the bookstores and book reviews, come up with some suggestions, and I'd like you to be one of the scouts. You've always been such a good participant."

"Rewarded by being given more to do. Sounds like my job."

Rozanne looked startled.

"Joke! Joke, you sensitive hostess. I would be glad to."

"Thanks. I know I got a little academic this time. We had

done novels the last three times and I thought some history might be a good change."

"It is a good change and you are a good person and your coffee cake is yummy."

"Tante Sirca made it."

"Tante Sirca?"

"Aunt Sara. As in Lee."

Others gathered around, thanked Rozanne, said goodbye.

When Carole got home she had to call Ernestine.

"Sister mine, you will not believe this. Believe it. You know that book club I've gone to?"

"The one Sukie also goes to?"

"Boy do I feel not smart. Sta-HOO-pid. You got it right away, but I sure didn't."

"You went and she was there?"

"Never occurred to me, never thought of it. Might have made some excuse. Or maybe be tough and go, but go prepared. Not dim bulb I. Just put on my happy face and strolled in and--"

"There she was."

"Too easy. Jamie cuts her finger, I have to get a bandage, so I'm running late. There Sukie was on a sweet little love seat, so precious, and guess where the only available seat was?"

"NO!"

"Oh but yes. There we are, sitting as far apart as we can on a piece of furniture designed to get two people together. Not even elbows touching, not for a moment."

"This is priceless."

"But something good came out of it, actually quite good."

"You accidentally spilled coffee on her. Down there."

"No violence, ever the lady. No, what happened is that I realized it is not the talk of the neighborhood. One of the others would have done something, arched her eyebrows or smirked or given us the evil eye--"

"Or fallen on the floor laughing."

"Or that. But nothing, not the least hint. I think they, you know, those two, they avoided detection."

"Except by you."

"Um, yeah, I stand corrected. Never forget that moment. But whatever time he spent with her after he moved out, they didn't broadcast it. I'm as sure as I can be no one knows."

"Didn't park in her driveway and shout 'Honey, I'm home'?"

"How can any sister of mine have such a weird sense of humor?"

"How can any sister of mine not realize Sukie was likely to participate in the same book club that she did pre-Kenneth?"

"Which brings us to another question--"

"Let me try. I think I can guess it."

"Yezzz?"

"Did Sukie draw a blank, the way my beloved but unaware sister did, or was she there on purpose. Confrontation."

"Maybe she didn't care. Brazen hussy, I think the term is. Didn't make a lick of difference if I was there or not."

"Real balls. Larry uses that as the universal compliment for anyone with lots of courage or gall or whatever. Men and women. Real balls, he says."

"Time to elevate this conversation. How's the family?"

"No colds, no tissues, health all around. Larry asks for Carole updates on a regular basis, wait till he hears this one! Thanks for the laugh. You keep having moments that should be captured on film."

"I live to amuse you."

"I love you. Said it first your bubble's burst."

"Later."

"Later."

Chapter Fourteen

Ken and Carole arrived at the office of Norman Jones, Mediator, for their second session. They both knew this had to be done, both accepted that a detailed plan about money and time and responsibility for Jamie would be essential to letting them get on with their lives without having to debate the cost of a new party dress or a medical expense or vacation plans. But it was painful, breaking time and money into cold little pieces, thinking about Jamie's expenses as if she were a house or pet to be maintained and cared for.

The process was also made difficult by the realization that the remaining time with her at home was so short, so very short. Norm asked if they wanted to have a preliminary discussion about college costs, not part of the agreement but a sharing of ideas. Carole and Ken declined, felt it was too early, and since there was a reasonable chance that Jamie could earn an academic scholarship, things could change a lot over the coming years. They did agree that it made sense to come back and begin mediating her educational expenses during her senior year, perhaps again during the college years. But although they did not spend much time on the question, the reality of their only child so soon to be grown and gone saddened both Ken and Carole, made them want to make the most, and best, of the remaining time with Jamie.

Ken came with three copies of everything he had prepared, and he handed one each to Norm and Carole. He had a notebook in which he frequently made notes and conducted himself in a terse but polite, calm manner. He looked at Carole only a few times, and slipped into a condescending tone twice but quickly got back to a flat, unemotional voice. So in control. Carole was outwardly calm, but upset and a little angry at Ken's style, the "let's get this unpleasant business over with" air he assumed. She was some warm, an Ernestine phrase.

They reached an agreement on the expenses for their child. Then they moved on to the question of time. Time with Dad. Time with Mom. Parsing of moments, fleeting moments. Both agreed that they could work out time with families for major holidays such as Christmas morning, Thanksgiving dinner. They agreed to cooperate on getting Jamie to birthday parties or school activities. Norm approved, said it was their agreement, and if they felt confident that holidays would not be a problem, could agree to agree, with a return to the mediation table always an option.

Structuring child-with-parent time was more difficult. Ken had taken an apartment only a mile and a half from his former residence, done so deliberately so that he could easily pick up his daughter from home or school. The weekends would alternate, weekend starting at five p.m. on Friday and ending at five p.m. on Sunday, the picking-up parent providing the transportation. The divorcing parents quickly agreed. Weekdays, though, were a problem.

"I want Jamie for dinner every Tuesday and Thursday."

"No."

"No?"

"Carole, Ken is proposing that he have dinner with Jamie every Tuesday and Thursday, a structure you've rejected. Please share with me your concerns with that proposal" said Norm. He took off his glasses and polished the lenses with his handkerchief.

"It's too disruptive, to her, to me. She has homework--"

"Not during the summer--"

"She has homework nine months of the year" Carole said, half turning toward Ken but not seeking his eyes, her voice tensing. "She is almost certainly going to play field hockey. And last week, out of the blue, she got out that clarinet." Carole turned back to Norm and explained "She wanted to take lessons when she was eight. Heard a clarinet at a concert, had to have it, took lessons for two years and gave it up. Last week she gets it out and tells me she wants to start again, that she's sorry she ever quit, wants to swing like Benny Goodman. Benny Goodman! My daughter constantly amazes me."

"Our daughter. I found that clarinet in New York, remember?"

"The *point* is that she is busy with homework and sports and maybe clarinet. She needs her sleep and I don't think she should have the middle of the week broken up. We've agreed to two weeks with you in the summer. Tell you what, if you want more than two weeks we can do that. If you want some middle-of-the-week days in the summer, sure. But not the school year. She has great grades and I don't want them to slip."

"I don't want them to slip either, dear" he said with a sarcastic delivery of the endearment. "But now you are being selfish, aren't you? I drop Jamie off on a Sunday night, and don't see her again until a week from the next Friday. Twelve days! Come on Carole, don't use her to punish me."

Norman Jones's instincts told him they were sharing points of view more than speech making, so he held back. Like all good mediators, he was often balanced on a point of decision; to be quiet so that a dialogue, rough but productive, could continue, or to interrupt and take control of a deteriorating situation.

Carole turned in her seat, then moved her chair so she was looking right at Ken. He looked down at his papers. Calmly, with her own light touch of condescension, she answered him. "I am not trying to punish you. I am trying to help our daughter, our daughter maintain her good grades and get the scholarship we talked about a few minutes ago. I also realize that she has other interests that take time, time away from home and homework. If she is riding in your car or my car she is not practicing clarinet or doing homework or running laps. Or going to sleep early. It just breaks up the evening too much."

"It takes less than ten minutes, door to door. So much for your riding time. I can pick her up at field hockey practices, take her to clarinet lessons, feed her a nutritious dinner. This is bullshit and you know it."

"Ken, can you offer a suggestion on how this might be resolved?" Norm said.

"I am not going twelve days without seeing my daughter. We can drop this right now, Carole. As they say in the movies, I'll see you in court. Speaking of which, you do know the standard rules for time-sharing, don't you? Did your lawyer tell you what the court will impose if we can't agree?"

"Yes, but it isn't good for her. For *her*."

"Rats, Norm, we were doing so well, but I think we just hit the old brick wall" Ken said, starting to gather his papers with dramatic effect.

"Mediators don't give up so easily, Ken. The manual says this is a classic time for a caucus, so let's caucus. To review the rules, I'm going to speak with each one of you privately, but not share anything either one said, and not bring anything back to the table unless you want me to. I'd like to start with Carole. Ken, please excuse us, and then I'll meet with you."

After Ken left, Norm stood up. "Mediation is good for the brain but bad for the body. Too much sitting." He walked to one wall of the office and leaned against it. "So what do we have?"

"My view?"

"Of course. What is your perspective, your view of the situation."

Carole sat for a few seconds, not talking. Norm waited. She got up, went to the one window and looked out, walked around the room, sat down. She sighed a great, weary sigh.

"He is right of course. Right because the court will impose one evening a week, my attorney already showed me the standard schedule, and right ---"

Another long moment. Norm went to the water cooler in the corner, took two paper cups and filled them, the air bubbles burbling up. He offered one to Carole.

"Thanks."

"You're welcome. Going to drop the other shoe?"

"He is right because he shouldn't go twelve days without seeing Jamie, and Jamie shouldn't go twelve days either."

"Would you like to offer something when we are back together?"

"Sure, one day, I mean one evening a week. Supper, a few hours, maybe pick her up after school or from a lesson. Or from the house, I don't care."

"You sound like you do care. I'm not trying to make you say or agree to anything, Carole."

"No, one evening will work, and she'll get her homework done. It's just, it's just---sorry, this isn't counseling. I have been avoiding going to a counselor for some time but I've got to get some stuff resolved."

"Do you have one? Would you like some names?"

"We went together to Dr. Ckeye, my failed attempt at marriage saving. I liked her, do you know her?"

"Only by reputation, but it's a good one. I always encourage counseling. Nothing is as good for healing and getting on with your life. Call her."

"I will. Ken must be chewing the furniture by now."

"Take the time you need. Is there anything else you want to say to me in caucus?"

"No, his turn. Nothing personal, Norm, but I really want to get out of here."

"Understood. Please trade places with Ken."

Ken came in and sat heavily in his chair. "Can I ask you something?"

"Sure, but I can't comment on what Carole shared."

"No, I know that. Just wondered how we're doing."

"Doing---"

"As clients. Mediatees, I guess."

"In terms of---"

"Cooperation. Success."

"Pretty good, pretty good, Ken. No swearing, well, a little, but no swearing at each other. No shouting, no accusing each other of every sin under the sun and moon. You've agreed to expenses relating to Jamie, your child, which is almost impossible for some couples, and quickly agreed to a holiday schedule. This is the first point you've been stuck on. So let me revise my rating. You are doing very well as a couple, far better than many. I'm counting on the two of you to jump this final hurdle so I can sleep the sleep of a successful mediator."

"I'm not going to agree to a twelve-day absence."

"Can you propose a schedule that addresses your wishes and Carole's concerns? One that works, is good for Jamie too."

"Once a week. One dinner hour a week, plus the weekend schedule we talked about. Hell, the county will give me that anyway, if I take her back to court," Ken concluded.

"You think that is fair, equitable, and works for Jamie."

"Why doesn't it?"

"Not debating you, Ken. That was a check, not a challenge. Let me restate it. You feel that you would be satisfied, comfortable, with an agreement that gave you the responsibility for Jamie every other weekend, Friday at five to Sunday at five, plus one night a week. You also feel that plan addresses Carole's concerns about Jamie's schoolwork and activities and will fit well for her. For Jamie."

"Yes, I really do. OK, what I'm going to propose is that one day a week I pick her up after school, dinner, homework time, home by nine. No, nine-thirty. I'll let Carole pick the day, although Wednesday seems reasonable, mid-week. And at least two weeks, solid, in the summer, but I want to think about that a bit, not ready to discuss it today. So just the week schedule for now. Schedule of weeks, I guess." He paused briefly. "Look, I am worried about Jamie telling me to get lost. Carole caught me with another woman, really trashy behavior on my part. I am grateful that she never told Jamie; but even without that, Jamie knows I'm the one who split -- it's my fault her parents aren't together. I have always been a pretty good dad, we get along fine, and I don't want to lose that. So if she needs to get to a lesson or a party or something, I will absolutely make sure she gets there if she's with me that day."

"Did you ever tell Carole you were grateful?"

"Right after we split, I asked her if she had told Jamie about me and Sukie. Carole said of course not or words to that effect."

"Did you thank her? Did you tell her you were grateful? I think she did the right thing, don't mistake me, I think it would have been a disservice to your daughter to give her that information; but lots of spouses would have. In fact, lots of spouses do."

"Well -- at the end of that conversation -- hard one, it was, I said thanks for not telling Jamie. But it was as I was leaving, not sure it registered. So you think I should thank her."

"Part of the mediation process is learning skills that come in handy later on. For instance, you talked about coming back to mediate college costs. That's fine, I'd be pleased to help, but perhaps you and Carole have learned something in these two sessions that you can use when the time comes. Maybe you will be able to sit down and work it out in a mutually respectful manner, and won't need me. Back to your question. I'm not going to offer an opinion on whether you should thank Carole for not telling Jamie about an affair you had. But I will offer this. You just said you were grateful. I think people should say 'please and thank you, I appreciate that, I am grateful for, I understand your point of view,' and similar phrases and sentiments as often as possible. And the hard-to-swallow words, 'I'm sorry' and 'I was wrong, I apologize.' I've seen those words pay dividends, great dividends."

Ken sat looking at Norm, slowly nodding his head. "I hear you."

"Are you ready to talk to Carole about the question at hand?"

"I am ready to see if she will agree to one day a week. Twice a week gets a no from her, and every other week gets a no from me. Sounds like the middle is the only place for us to go. And I think the summertime question is one we can work out, I don't think Carole will object to two or three weeks. Probably not."

"Anything else you want to address before we get back together?"

"No."

Norm went to the door, opened it and invited Carole to return and be seated. He then walked around the table to his chair and sat, folding his hands on the table. "Anyone have any offer to make?"

A brief pause, and then Ken said "How about one evening a week? Wednesdays if possible. I will pick her up from school or home, depending on my schedule, and have her home by nine-thirty. An afternoon, dinner, homework time with the TV off and me quietly reading. That's all. And if she has a test we can get take-out, quick meal, and she can study while I read, or I can quiz her. Honey, I want her to do well as much as you do."

They both ignored the force of habit "Honey."

"I agree."

"And two, maybe three weeks in the summer. I'm thinking we can work that out, agree on -- agree on some weeks. To be discussed, OK?"

"To be discussed, but two weeks sounds reasonable. Maybe three."

Norm tilted his head. "Sounds like you two have reached an agreement, weekends as already described, and one evening a week as Ken just offered. What I suggest is that I send a copy in a few days to each of you about the agreement you've reached, and to each of your lawyers, unless you want to do that yourself, in which case I will send you two copies." He paused a moment, pointed to his stacks of papers and the filled easel sheets pinned to the walls and still on the easels. "I take such detailed notes, and double check each point with you, so that when I type it all up I get everything right. However, I certainly may get a point wrong, so please call me at once and I will correct it and rush changes to you. If something bothers you, or your attorneys, we can get together again, but it seems to me that you have voluntarily designed an agreement, a structure, that works for both of you and for your child. Some weeks in the summer when Jamie is with Ken full time is yet to be discussed, but you've both indicated that is a discussion you're willing to have. And, as I said when we first met, if you wish I would be pleased to mediate the division of your assets and liabilities."

Ken and Carole both said that sending a copy directly to their attorneys would be fine, and that they would certainly consider his offer of additional services.

"I love this part of being a mediator. I sometimes wish I could throw confetti, but that might not seem professional. Let me say, however, that I congratulate you both on the cooperation and understanding you showed each other in reaching a mediated agreement, always keeping Jamie in mind.

"Thank you" said Carole, starting to rise.

"Please, just one moment, Carole. Please. Yes, thanks, Norm, well done. This was a lot easier than I thought it would be, didn't need to bring all those ledger sheets, did I?" He turned in his chair, looked at Carole. She turned and for the first time that evening they made eye contact.

"I want to say that I am grateful that you didn't tell Jamie Sue about Sukie, about any of it. You could have, and it would have made things harder for me with the kid, a lot harder. Thank you."

"I did it for her, not for you. But you're welcome."

They shook Norm's hand and walked out together. They wished each other goodnight.

Chapter Fifteen

The county courthouse was completed in 1873, a magnificent edifice that reflected the nineteenth century wealth of greater Boston and much of New England -- money from shipbuilding and fishing along the coast, farming in the fertile soil of Massachusetts. Through the over one-hundred years since its construction there had been several changes. Electricity of course, installed around the turn of the century -- improvements in plumbing and public restroom facilities, a small elevator shoehorned into a corner of the building, recording devices and television cameras. But modernization did not change the overall look, the feel of the building. It projected an image that it had existed, and would exist, practically forever.

The divorce hearing was set for one-thirty. Carole had taken a half-day personal leave, not being sure how long it would take or how she would feel when it was over. Trudy had offered to be with her, share a drink after. Carole thanked her but declined, not wishing to invest the procedure with any more ceremony than necessary, so she went to work as usual, got caught up in the flow and worked until noon. Although she did not feel hungry, she stopped in the lobby of her office building and got an Energy Booster shake from the kiosk. The mixture of ice, yogurt, strawberries, bananas, and protein powder was cold, and Carole had to sip it slowly as she got in her car and drove the few miles to the courthouse, parking on the top level of a nearby three-story garage. She sat in her car and finished the shake, walked down the three flights of stairs and threw the container in a trashcan at the exit.

The courthouse grounds were beautifully maintained, flowers in abundance throughout the growing season, the walks diligently cleared of snow and ice in winter. There were flowering bushes and evergreens, and a few stately red leaf oaks that were older than the gray stone building they shaded. There were statues and plaques honoring young men, and a few young women, lost in the Revolutionary, Civil, Spanish-American, and all the wars since. The county decorated these commemoratives with flags and flowers, not only on national holidays but often throughout the year. Encouraged by this, people brought their own flowers and ribbons and tokens, fewer and fewer over the years at the WWII memorial, but still some -- many at the Korean and Vietnam memorials.

Inside the courthouse it was comfortable yet dramatic, all dark polished wood, brass, stone. The corridors were wide, ceilings high, with filigreed woodwork produced by skilled craftsmen long ago. The steps were white marble with blue and gray veins, as if a fine blue cheese were cast in stone. The millions of footsteps on that marble over the years had eroded slight depressions in the steps, gentle hollows like a path through a pasture.

It was a few minutes after one. Carole went to the restroom and then sat on a high-backed wood bench across from a door with "Courtroom C Judge Doris Skalen" written in gold leaf on the frosted window. In the wide corridor there were people standing and talking or walking with purpose -- clerks and attorneys and police officers and people with business before the court or one of the many bureaus in the building. Carole's attorney, Sophie Bertinski, had promised to meet her about one-fifteen. Everything had been agreed to in the previous weeks, so they had nothing to rehearse.

As she sat there she heard voices and looked down the hall to see Ken and his attorney walking toward her. They stopped near the doorway. Carole glanced down the hall in both directions but did not see Sophie. She didn't know what to do with her eyes, her face. Carole didn't want to look at Ken but didn't want to make a show of not looking at him. And since he was in front of her on the far side of the wide corridor she would have to turn her head or move to another bench to not have him in her field of vision. Carole wished she had a newspaper with her, wide pages to open and shake and use as a shield. She saw Ken say something to his attorney and then leave him, starting to walk directly towards her. Carole put her head down, staring at her lap, held up her right hand then both hands as stop signs, slowly shaking her head "No." Ken stopped, stood a moment and then reversed his course. Carole heard the click of heels on the hard tile floor and was relieved to look down the hall and see Sophie walking briskly toward her. She came to Carole and sat next to her after disconnecting herself from a purse, shoulder bag and thin briefcase.

All the many months it had taken to get to this point, and here it was, she was Getting Divorced. First a few moments talking to her attorney, the papers neat and formal containing the mediated agreement. Then she found herself in the august courtroom telling the judge that she did want a divorce, that she agreed to the parenting agreement for Jamie, while in her head she was saying she did not want to be Getting Divorced, her heart is broken beyond the judge's understanding.

Like water down a drain, slowly then suddenly swirling and finished, Carole Tagee was no longer a wife. She watched herself agree, watched herself sign the papers, just doing it. As it was ending she realized that Ken was no longer wearing his wedding band, and she wondered when he had removed it. She thought of taking hers off and flinging it at him, or dropping it bouncing ringing on the floor, but did neither.

Carole and Sophie spoke a few moments then parted.

As Carole was leaving the courthouse she saw a row of pay phones and briefly considered calling Trudy at work, asking if she could get away for that drink. But she didn't feel like being cheered up or told to be strong, and certainly didn't want small talk. What she wanted, needed, was to be very busy, and she also briefly considered returning to work. What she chose was to go home and clean.

Going to wash that man right out of my hair! Well said! Carole took off her clothes, put on old jeans and a sweatshirt declaring her support of NPR and began to assemble dust mop, cloths, bucket, sponges, bottles of products to make everything new again. As she started to pull on her bright yellow rubber gloves she looked at her wedding band and engagement ring. A few drops of soap and water, some twisting and pulling, and they were off. In the trash? Couldn't do that -- could be wrapped in a paper towel and stuck in the bottom of a deep dresser drawer containing thick wool sweaters.

The dust bunnies never had a chance. Carole not only cleaned under the beds but carefully vacuumed the bottoms of the box springs and the bed legs and wheels in their coasters. She washed and wiped, waxed and polished, so when her back began to twinge a bit she felt good about quitting because so much had been accomplished.

Bubble bath? Why not. Soaking in the tub Carole almost fell asleep. Later, starved but in no mood to cook or have to clean up, she and Jamie went out for dinner and had a great time. As Carole had promised, two cool ladies. Two very cool ladies.

Chapter Sixteen

Ralph had promised himself no more blind dates, but doubted he would keep that promise. He was so unsure of himself and his emotions. Often he was consumed by the urge to find perfect person, the same belief in go-steady get-married he had held since he first discovered girls. Other times he was torn and ashamed and scared of being wrong in love again. The Cassie experience had been such a -- disappointment seemed a weak word, too weak to describe the end of a short-lived marriage. But it was exactly that. Ralph expected to be married once, forever. A bowl full of disappointment indeed, with side orders of embarrassment and pain.

Tom Lagrinka, happily married Tom, kept trying to find a woman for his buddy "-- great as my Gracie!" Tom would report that he and Gracie had sex last night or last weekend. "Really cranked it up, we did" he would say, while the two men trundled down the fairway at the city golf course. No details, for which Ralph was glad, but it did get to him. It was that same combination of voyeurism and envy he felt in high school about those who had bragged about their exploits, even minor ones "-- inside the bra!"

So here they were again, playing golf according to their own rules based on a love of getting out and hacking the ball around and smoking a cigar and drinking a few beers afterward.

The rules: Move the ball as much as necessary to get a clear shot. If trapped behind a tree or in deep rough there is a choice -- hack out of the rough or from behind the tree if you want to, throw it onto the fairway if the tree has you completely blocked or the rough is too rough (always say "Oh shit" or "Fuck it" when taking ball-throwing liberties), and never, never keep score.

The one part of the game that followed traditional rules was putting. A throwback to their youth, pre-driver's license days, when they would take the bus to the Northpark Amusement Center and play serious miniature golf -- the putting was done in silence, with appropriate ceremony. They exalted when the long putt made and grieved over the missed three-footer and gave each other a "cool" or "nice putt" when the ball dropped. But no scores.

The rest of the game was as casual as the putting was serious, although of course one didn't talk during the actual windup and delivery of the club to the ball. So Tom waited until Ralph had whacked a drive off the fifth tee – 520 yards par five dogleg right with traps at the elbow of the dogleg – before saying "Yuhknow -- the one I told you about that was getting divorced? Remember, I told you I told her I know this great guy but she said not till she was divorced? Anyhoo, so now she is and you know she ain't had any for about a year. I mean, think about it, early thirties, gettin' it regular, marriage goes to shit, she gets divorced, lawyers take forever, needs some manhood attention, what? Nice tits, too."

"Face?"

"Yeah, she has a face."

"Which looks like?"

Tom didn't answer, he was going through his pre-drive ritual. He hitched up his khaki shorts, tugged at his oversize Green Bay Packers shirt, and wiped his hands on his shorts, two permanent stains from the thousands of wipings no washing could remove. Finally he took the club back, gave it that double-hitch that no doubt contributed to his uncertain results, and hit a drive that went higher and shorter than Tom would have liked, although it did stay on the fairway.

Ralph grabbed his bag and started walking towards his ball, further than Tom's in the short rough to the left. "So she's bat-shit ugly, but has nice tits and you figure she needs it."

"No, numbnuts, she is not bat-shit ugly. Kinda cute, in fact I'd pop her myself if I weren't so happily married."

"And the clear fact that Gracie would cut your cock off should such popping take place."

"Uh, yeah."

At this point they parted. Tom was away so he hit first, a long fine hook to the left as the course doglegged right. Into the trees. Ralph, dressed as usual in painter's pants -- lots of room for the balls, human and golf -- found his ball slightly buried in weedy grass, and he might have kicked it out until he saw where Tom's went. So he smacked it with a seven iron and it moved down the fairway a reasonable distance. Then Ralph walked over to see if Tom needed help finding his ball. But no, it was sitting on a little pool of dry brown pine needles, and there was an opening onto the fairway.

"Yeah, but, no really she is decent to look at, sorta blond hair, nice tits, OK, yuhknow? And even with real smarts. Hellofa money manager. I could fix you up, we could double or something, or maybe you just want I should tell her there is this guy, kind of a jerk, but he wants to screw you, and see if she says yes."

"You are sooo crude. I keep hoping Gracie will shape you up, but it's probably not going to happen."

"Probably not going to happen."

"OK, I will break my pledge to myself to give up on the blind dates, but if this flunks then I am going to do that videotape matchmaking thing. Maybe out of sympathy you'll pay for it."

Enough talk. Time for golf. "Hero shot" Tom said, getting out his three iron. "Wieskopf is over the ball, with a good shot here he can hold onto his one stroke lead and win the U. S. Open. The crowd is absolutely silent."

"The crowd is bored by the bullshit" said Ralph.

Tom gave him the fuckyou look, took back the club, double clutched just a little -- an iron, not a driver, after all -- and really smacked it, hit one of his best shots in a long time. The ball bounced on the green about ten feet past the hole and spun back about seven and though they didn't keep score they both knew he was looking at a possible birdie, rare in their golf outings. Ralph gave him high praise, "Lucky fuck," and went to his ball. He tried the same technique, a quick hit, and pulled the club across his body, missed the green and the trap and the short rough but put it almost out of play, about thirty yards to the left of the pin. Tom did not comment. He was getting into the idea of a birdie and had on his serious face.

Ralph went to his ball and found it deep in thick grass. He tried to chip it out with a sand wedge but dropped his shoulder and just buried the club in the dirt, moving the ball about three inches. He immediately whacked it again, lifting his shoulder this time and opening up the club face, rocketing the ball across the green to the other side whereupon Ralph walked over, picked up his ball, and said "Next hole, Mr. Wieskopf."

Tom stood over his putt, irked that his hands were more than usually sweaty. If he wiped them, not on his pants but with the golf towel, he would have to suffer grief. But he really wanted to sink it. He put down his putter and walked over to his bag to get his towel.

Ralph, in partial violation of the "Putting is sacred" rule, began to half sing the old rock song Tighten Up, "Do the Tighten Up, yeah do the Tighten Up."

Tom ignored him, picked up the club, the singing stopped of course, and he sank the putt. Silence from Ralph, the highest compliment. Tom gave himself a loud "You da MAN," complete with bent knee and arm pump.

Over beers in the clubhouse the subject of the blind date came up again. Ralph turned down the idea of the double date. If it is wrong, better wrong for a short time, easier to end the evening. He chose, or rather offered that she choose, lunch or after-work drink.

"You don't get it, my boy" said Tom, a touch of the W. C. Fields in his voice. "This is a sure thing, a slam dunk, or slam probe, a lady so full of deeeeesire that even you can get home on this one. Or do beauty and brains intimidate you?"

"Could it be you are wrong? Could it be? Like, maybe the lady is angry at men, or scared, or thinking of trying women. Lots of options other than--"

"Ready to rumble. Hot to trot."

"As long as we're friends I'll never lose touch with high school. That's the deal, turkey, quick lunch or quick drink -- the lady's choice, and don't be surprised if she says she doesn't want a blind date. I don't want a blind date, she doesn't want a blind date, a perfect combination. We can avoid each other to our hearts' content."

Tom drew himself up with an indignant air, belched loudly, and said "I will convey your chicken-shit, limp-dick request to the lady in question. Now buy me a beer for taking care of your love life."

"Exactly wrong. You buy me a beer, and if she is willing to see me I'll buy you two beers. And didn't your mother ever tell you to say 'excuse me'?"

"And if you get laid on the first date you can buy me an eighteen ounce porterhouse, medium rare, onion rings." Tom banged his fist on the table and tried to belch again, but the fizz was gone.

"And if I don't score, you buy me one?"

"Sad, sad, sad. Should you fail, then it is obvious you have no moves at all. If you can't charm a long-lonely widow by divorce, forget you."

Chapter Seventeen

Carole had skipped a week to be with Jamie, but returned to the women's group the second week. She said hello to Judy and the other familiar faces, a few of which she was able to greet by name. She remembered Rhonda, and asked her how the child care venture was coming.

"Still thinkin', talkin' about it, but I think it's gonna happen. You got little kids?"

"No" smiled Carole, "But I might have some leads for you. Good luck."

Judy called them together, introduced two newcomers, both named Linda, and asked if anyone had anything to share.

"I have a hassle to share" said Janice.

"Hassle sharing, hassle sharing" said several of the women in approximate unison.

"Please, always say your name first time each evening."

"Right, Judy. I been coming long enough I should have that down. OK, I'm Janice. Hello Linda and Linda. OK, hassle sharing. I'm a little embarrassed. We share so many hassles about not enough money, but mine is about -- "

"Too much? Easy. Send it to me" laughed one of the new Lindas.

"Well, not too much, but new money. More money."

"This sounds like it may be one of our happier hassles" said Judy.

"Well, when we got divorced he had an apartment, paying rent, of course still a mortgage on the house for me and the kids, so we worked out child support. It wasn't much but really all he could afford. Poor guy had almost no moneys to chase the honeys." This brought out comments of "Ain't it sad" and "Tell him to find a rich one" to general laughter.

"I was a teller at the bank, getting around 25 to 30 hours. My ex was making about 35 thousand, so it was tough with two households and four kids. Sometimes real tough. But my kids were little and I needed to be home a lot, the older ones helped some but, well, they were eight, no, nine, eight, five and three when we split. So the older kids couldn't do a lot, just make toast or cereal or microwave something, do a load of whites, you know. But now the oldest are twelve and almost eleven, good kids, they really help out, I tell them all the time how much they help, how much I appreciate it." No comments from the others, but several nodded their heads in firm agreement. "And the little ones aren't so little, my baby's in first grade, I can't believe it! So the bank made me a full time teller about a year ago, and two months ago I got assistant head teller, I think I forgot to share that."

"Congratulations!"

"Good for you!" came from several of the members.

"--and my ex got a big promotion, district manager. He travels some but not too much. So his schedule is all different but we can work out the visits, that's not hard to figure. But now we together make about seventy, used to have forty-seven or forty-eight thousand a year between us, seventy seems like a fortune."

"You sure you got a hassle, honey?" from Jolyn drew laughter and requests from others that they suffer the same fate.

"Well, here is the hassle, not a big problem, I guess, but things aren't smoother between me and my ex, even with more money, because before it was all worked out. You know, what he would pay, what I would, our lawyers figured it out, it was fair. But now he spends some extra sometimes, sometimes I do, and the kids want more. New clothes, better clothes. Clothes with labels. Toys, new bikes, stuff. Stuff!" Janice said the last words with open hands and a big, encompassing gesture to more appreciative laughter.

"So now we need new rules. He didn't before argue about clothes 'cause we had a rule about it. But now the kids want better, don't want to shop in the discount store and I'll never get them to the second-hand shop again. Well, now my ex gives more dollars but an opinion with each buck. Like a comment a dollar, you know? 'Why are you buying designer labels? Can't you wait for sales? The kids don't need all this stuff, you're just pissing away the money.' My ex is a great one for giving advice. And I'm thinking, first, the kids and me, and *me*, deserve better; and second, I do buy things on sale and discount, but I don't always want the kids to know. Usually don't tell them. I got some fancy jeans half price because the cuff was hemmed wrong at the factory, took me ten minutes a cuff to fix them, did it at night after the kids were asleep. The next morning they were all 'Wow, thanks Mom, cool jeans!' you know? But if I told my turkey ex they were from the seconds bin he'd tell them in a shot. I know him, never misses a chance to get the kids down on me. So I figure better he thinks I'm pissing away his money than the kids do their sad act. 'Don't give me that poverty pout' I tell them. I'm sorry, am I taking too much time? I'm ready to ask for advice now."

"Please, take the time you need, we are all ears and ready advice" said Judy.

"So like I said, what we need are new rules that work like the old rules when we didn't have as much money. Actually the old rules are still around, but the extra dollars don't fit, you know? But I'm not crazy about starting that lawyer thing again. All that back and forth takes time, costs a lot. Those lawyers start talking to each other and they both got their meters running. And over what? Clothes, shoes, maybe a vacation. You know -- how to spend the money we have now that we didn't have then. How to spend it on the kids."

"Have you tried mediation?"

"Name, please," said Judy softly.

"Sorry. Carole. Mediation might be just the answer. I, we, used it for a time agreement, who and when our daughter is with mom or dad, plus some basic money agreements. We might go back and mediate the money some more, but for now everything is working OK. But I understand the process enough to know it works really well when you're trying to deal with numbers. Money. You want a new monthly figure for clothes, you work it out at the table together, no back-and-forth except right there, right then. Once you get that worked out you don't have to justify each purchase."

"Can you share some experiences with mediation that you have had, Carole?"

"It isn't exactly the same situation, we only have one child, Jamie, and our jobs haven't changed. But I guess the important thing is not the differences but that we too had money and time, parenting rules, to discuss. We went to this mediator, I'll give you his name, and he really made it easy. Well, easier. He had these forms, we talked about them, filled them out at home and came back and worked it out. About four hours, that's all it took, the homework helped a lot, saved time. He charged one-fifty an hour, total, not each, so seventy-five an hour each and done in two meetings. But, and here I am repeating what he said several times, the important thing is not the savings in time or money, although those do happen, but that we get to design the package. It is our agreement. We worked it out, and if either one of us said no then there was no deal. Of course, hanging over our heads is that if we couldn't agree we would have to start all over with our lawyers, but what we came up with was what we wanted. The mediator guided us, kept us in the middle, asked reality-check questions. I recommend it and recommend him.

"I'm Jolyn. What were the forms?"

"Who pays for what. All kinds of things are listed -- clothes, shoes, summer camp, medicine, health insurance, almost everything you can think of to spend money on for children. And space to add other items. Special things like horseback riding lessons, unusual expenses. Another form is holidays, every one of them, all the religions and their big events. Christmas and Easter for us, but it also asked about Jewish and Muslim and some other religions, so you respond to the ones that fit, that you celebrate. And all the birthdays, national holidays. So I filled out one and Ken, that's his name, Ken, he filled out one and then we got together. Some were easy. For instance, I get health insurance cheaper than Ken does, so I carry our daughter. We could have traded off that expense for something else, but Ken offered to write me a check every quarter for half the cost. I do most of the clothes shopping -- actually Jamie does it and I supply the plastic, so we left it that way and he's going to pay some child support. He would rather write checks, and I like it that way because I know what is coming in each month or quarter. So we both are pretty happy with the agreement."

"Hi. I'm one of the new Lindas. Thanks for having this group, by the way. This is my first time and I'm already glad I came. So can you tell me what'd you work out about holidays? I mean, I'm married, hope we can keep it together, but it sure ain't easy. Thanksgiving's always a tug-and-pull at our place. His witch of a mother, who I swear glared at me during our wedding, wants our kids at her house every time. That's it. Period. Like the only Thanksgiving is her Thanksgiving, where else could the children possibly go? Not stay home with me and my family, oh no! So we have two meals, or only her meal, or visit my family but don't eat much. I love my hubby, but when his mother handed him over to me she kept his balls at home."

"Maybe one ball, you do have children, don't you?" Rhonda asked to general laughter.

"Maybe one, but thatun's only on loan. I don't want to

fight with him, but every Thanksgiving is a teeth-grinder. Tell you the truth, her turkey is always dry. Got to ladle on the gravy. I know what she's doing wrong but I sure as hell won't tell her."

"Sure, we worked out holidays too," said Carole. "His birthday, my birthday, those were easy. Jamie's, we agreed to share. Thanksgiving is an alternate year thing, but that could change when she goes to college. And we didn't work out everything, like Fourth of July or New Years. Some people need more structure, some less, depends on how mad they are at each other, I guess. Maybe you could mediate Thanksgiving at your house every-other year in return for cooking lessons for your mother-in-law."

"I'd throw in smiling lessons. The witch."

The discussion stayed on this track for the rest of the session -- comments and questions about lawyers, mediators, the domestic court system, in-laws, shared parenting rules and responsibilities and costs and problems. At the end Carole gave Linda the mediator's name and number. Unlike the first session when she mostly listened, Carole was pleased to have been able to contribute, to offer help. She realized she was getting stronger, healing, and she left the meeting feeling fine.

Chapter Eighteen

Ralph Donnell assumed that people with names like Smith, Jones, West, Brown, must take for granted -- another one, Grant -- that their names would be spelled correctly, probably never thought about it and were astounded when mail came with misspellings. Donnell, however, was wrong so often that he always helped—"This is Ralph Donnell, two Ns, two Ls" -- but he still got Donel and Donal and Donald and even McDunnel and, of course, McDonald.

Ralph had always wanted to go steady. Ralph wanted one girl, wanted to be in love, felt that way from an absurdly early age. He just did -- not for any reason that he could discover, or wanted to discover, since he really liked feeling that way. His parents were happily married and had lots of happily married friends -- at least they seemed so to him when he was a little boy. By the time teenagehood came around, and he could see cracks in the relationships of the grownups around him, it was too late. By then he wanted one to love, a conviction of feelings that never changed.

The downside of this yearning for onegirl was that he rushed headlong into a marriage his second year of college, just turned twenty, and they were so perfectly mismatched. Cassie. It lasted barely a year. The divorce and serious blues that went along with ending their marriage -- a dissolution really because they had few assets and no children -- dragged down his studies so badly that he had to drop out to keep from flunking out. He gave up the apartment, moved back home, and buried himself in work, both to save money to go back to college. The work was also to avoid yearning for Cassie and confronting his sadness and shattered onegirl dream. Ralph spent the next two years working part-time at Sears a few nights and every weekend, selling power tools hand tools lawnmowers garden equipment, plus working full time in a steel fabrication factory.

"The first month he ached all the time and slept as many hours as he could; but after that, he started to grow muscles and soon felt physically in the best shape of his young life. When he was ready to return to school, he got a small college loan, moved out and into a simple apartment he shared with a graduate student, and graduated 30 months later with excellent grades.

Carole was raised by loving parents -- Smokey and Susan Preater -- a father who helped companies design advertising and promotional campaigns and a mother who worked part time at a library. Carole's earliest memories were of books and more books. There were always books in her room and her parents' room. Her parents wrestled with what to name her, wanting something a little unusual but not too, and so they chose Carole, the e making it slightly uncommon, as they wished. When her mother was expecting the second time, soon after Carole turned two, they decided on Ernest or Ernestine, partly in honor of Hemingway but also because it fit the "slightly unusual" criteria. It was a girl, dark haired rather than Carole's light brown but with the same deep brown eyes. They named her Ernestine, immediately Ernie. On her fourteenth birthday she announced her name was Ernestine, not Ernie, and corrected everyone until Ernie faded away almost totally.

The sisters were always best friends. There was the usual sibling rivalry, but these were incidents, not the overall pattern. As they grew, they grew closer.

Between the births of the two girls the family bought a new home near Boston. It was a spacious three bedroom in one of those neighborhoods with winding streets and cul-de-sacs designed so that a cluster of homes shared a large, common backyard. Of course everyone knew where lot lines were and mowed accordingly, but the kids just ran and rambled from swing-set to play-set, backdoor patio to backdoor patio, house to house.

Since Carole was the first she was given the bigger bedroom, wallpaper of pink flowers with little white lace bows. Because Ernest, or Ernestine, was not yet conceived, Smokey and Susan chose as wallpaper a gentle plaid, soft blue and pink and yellow, fit for either sex. The room was smaller than Carole's with part of the ceiling angling down with the roofline, making it the cozier of the two rooms, and so it became the sisters' favorite place for secrets and plotting and growing-up talk.

Ernestine got married about six months before Carole, both nice weddings. Their father, a man who loves his wife and daughters totally and without reservation, never said a word about the double whammy of paying for two weddings not long after paying for two college educations. They, mother as well as father, felt it was good and proper and quite wonderful to have two educated, married, happy children. Worth the price and more.

Ernestine married a civil engineer, Larry Myter, and a year after the marriage he was offered a wonderful job in Philadelphia, an opportunity that would almost certainly lead to part ownership of the firm. Boston and Philadelphia are not that far apart, but it certainly is not the same as living in the same town, and the sisters grieved some. They soon settled into phone calls about once a week, pictures mailed on occasion, and understanding husbands agreeing to visits four or five times a year. At first most of the visits were Ernestine and Larry coming to Boston, that being "Home," the place of parents and friends. In addition, Carole and Ken had a baby daughter, Jamie, so it was easier for the childless couple to travel. But they were trying to have children. One night, up too late at Carole and Ken's house, the four of them drank red wine and, tired and slightly tipsy, started talking about the euphemism "trying to have children" and talking about what it meant to try, and were they really trying, and other foolishness. They had a wonderful, silly conversation, laughing like crazy. Both sisters agree that Ernestine became pregnant that night, because Maxwell was born almost exactly nine months later, to be followed one year later by the twins, Samantha and Angelica, always Sammie and Angie.

Carole and Ken had never planned on having many children, maybe three. But Carole lost one early and then had terrible problems producing Jamie. It was a blessing that there were no physical or mental problems visited on Jamie as a result of her mother's difficult pregnancy, which included bleeding and other scary signs. The doctors strongly advised that she not have any more children, and she took the necessary medical steps to comply.

The couple were comfortable with the fact that they would have only one child, more so as she grew to be a bright, energetic child with a love of books and movies. The cousins looked forward to visits and played together with great energy and intrigue.

Chapter Nineteen

Tom felt no hesitation about trying to connect his two friends. What could be more natural than having two people he liked meet up and see if they liked each other. So the Monday after talking to Ralph he planned on getting this fix-up going just as quickly as possible. He got to his desk and followed his usual routine which consisted of taking off his jacket, hanging it on the wooden hanger with his black-markered name, sitting in his chair just a few moments to reacquaint himself with the most recent projects, then getting some coffee. Coffee in hand, he strolled down the aisle to Carole's spacious cubicle.

Carole kept her area as neat as possible. That was not easy since she seemed to be at the end of an open pipe of paper that she was always filing or filling out and sending back or pitching, taking a deep breath and then turning around to catch another face-full of paper from the pipe. It never stopped -- just slowed on occasion. Vacations were fine until she returned to the stacks waiting for her, papers murmuring "Read me first. Do me first." In front of her, just to the right of the computer, had been a picture of Ken -- a space since filled by a small clock and tape dispenser, so no hole was there to remind her of the missing picture or husband.

"Hey, Carole."

"Hey, Tom."

"So I gave your name to Ralph Donnell, my number one favorite golfing buddy, and he is going to call you. Let me tell you this is one great guy, OK?" He gave a half wave and turned to leave.

"Time out." He stopped moving, turning his head but not his body toward her. "Those wonderful sports phrases work every time. Come back here! Exactly when did I give you permission to offer my name up to your golfing buddies? And what makes you think I want a date on the recommendation of a man who loves his putter more than his wife?"

"I am so wounded! Poor me! And I ever gave you that impression? My wife I love far more than my putter -- not sure about my titanium driver that cost twice what I told Gracie it did. That I may love more than her. But no, this is a good guy who will take you out and be such a gentleman and not talk about sports more than maybe half the time. So he should call you at work or at home?"

"Any chance you will take no for an answer?"

Tom came back into her space, sat in one of the two blue guest chairs and started to set down his coffee cup. Carole grabbed one of the coasters she kept handy on her desk, sliding it in place just as the cup descended. He blinked, then remembered his manners. "So you want me to get you a coffee?" Carole shook her head slightly. "Don't change the subject. What will it take for you to leave both of us alone, old matchmaker?"

"I choose to accept the word 'old' as meaning expert and experienced, not a reference to my yet-tender age. And he not only doesn't want me to leave him alone, he looks to me as a dear friend, wise in the ways of women, donchaknow." Carole made a face, and leaned back. She had ordered a new chair recently, one that had lumbar support. "Now just lighten up, I wouldn't do wrong by either of you. This is a good match." Seeing she was about to object to that, he hurried on. "OK, no match, no match, sorry, just a good date. He buys you a drink, you drink the drink, you both talk about how divorce is a mess."

Carole stayed leaning way back in her new chair, now crossing her arms. "This gets better and better. He spends way too much on golf equipment, which he justifies by spending way too much time on the course, which broke up his first marriage, which makes him the perfect candidate for me. You are so very kind, but I will pass."

Tom put his feet up on a box marked "Financial Records, do not destroy until ___", with the date line blank. He looked smug, like she had walked into his trap.

"Actually, he was married short time to some kid while still in college. Two kids thinkin' they were adults, big mistake, and he is over that and all grown up and such a catch." He abruptly sat up, took up his coffee cup and walked out, saying "He'll call soon," and was gone before she could call another time out.

Ralph said he didn't want any more blind dates. He had told Tom that and meant it, but it was impossible to resist Tom's robust and raunchy optimism. So now it was time to make the call. Ralph sat at his desk, doodling squares, then triangles, hesitating about calling Carole. He hated it, hated the whole blind date thing. The calling and arranging and where do you meet? And then the big fear, the Five Minute Fear -- five minutes into the date he knows, or she knows, they *both* know that it is a mistake, ain't never going to happen, but there you are. There you are, dressed up, clean and smelling good, being pleasant with someone you're never going to see again, making small and smaller talk. Ralph sighed a little, started to pick up the phone, and it rang. Annoyed and relieved at the same time, he dealt with the call, a policy question, and then hung up. He picked up the piece of paper that Tom had given him, a subscription application card from Sports Illustrated with Carole's name and phone number written sideways on the edge, then picked up the phone and pushed the buttons for Carole's office.

"Carole Tagee."

"Hello, this is Ralph Donnell."

"Oh, hello, Ralph." Her voice was open and friendly, not revealing a powerful impulse to tell him this was too soon too soon, she just couldn't and hang up. Carole did not hang up, but, instead, focused on the company logo on her mouse pad. She sat bent slightly at the waist and stared at the blue-red-yellow-green twisted arrows symbol.

At his end of the phone line, Ralph leaned way back in his chair, feet straight out in front, pointing toes stretching and said "I assume Tom made as hard a sale on you as he did on me."

"Well, he did want us to meet, insisted on it."

Pause.

They both said, almost together, "So when do you want to meet?"

They each stumbled a bit, Ralph recovering first. "Lunch. How about lunch, or, if you prefer, a drink after work. Or dinner and a drink. Or just dinner. Aren't I smooth?"

Carole laughed, sat up in her chair, relaxed a bit. "Lunch is fine. Do you know Bistro Roma? Is that OK, not too far to go? How is next -- uh, next Wednesday? No? Thursday? Noon? All right, I'll be the lady with light brown hair looking lost."

Now Ralph laughed. "Please get a table if you get there first. I'll do the same. I look forward to meeting you." Ralph gently slapped his head with his free hand, wincing slightly from the words, not the slap. "Again with the smooth. I look forward to meeting you -- a living form letter."

"No, it's fine, I look forward to meeting you too."

They both said goodbye, again almost at the same moment, and hung up.

To be early? To be late? Ralph worried about that, decided to make sure he was on time by leaving the office early just in case, and sometimes cabs were hard to find. So of course the elevator was just opening on his floor as he got to it, going down. All aboard were heading to the lobby for the lunch hour, and as he walked outside a cab pulled up and dropped off a passenger and was his. Just like that. He got to the restaurant twenty-five minutes early. He got out of the cab and walked across the street to a small bookstore, stepped inside and picked up a book, looking sideways out the window. He felt a part of a Hitchcock movie, films he loved, so he pretended to browse and read while keeping an eye on the restaurant door. Cary Grant couldn't have done it better.

Ralph hoped that this woman, this Carole Tagee, would be someone he could enjoy dating, get serious about, get serious with. For over three years he had been sporadically dating Carmen -- that is, they took turns losing interest. Sometimes he would call her, sometimes she calling him. She would ask if he wanted to go on a day-t, two syllables, hard "T." Carmen is a woman with a sultry name, but rather than an olive-skinned Spaniard, she is a thin somewhat nervous natural blonde. From time to time Ralph has to attend client-sponsored parties, and for those events Carmen is a great date, or day-t. He could drop her off in the middle of a group of strangers doing the cheese cube and wine glass thing and go talk shop with clients. Later he could circle back and pick her up, happily chatting with men and women about the weather and shopping and men and her job and their jobs -- a real gift for high-quality small talk. The sex was also sporadic, but fine when it happened. She had a habit of making rabbit ears, quotation marks in the air, that always annoyed him and sometimes drove him nuts. Carmen could throw a pair of rabbit ears in the air every other sentence, several times a verbal paragraph. He could never marry her -- aside from the fact that he didn't love her, he was sure the rabbits would drive him to drink, or worse. "Well, your Honor, there we were, at the edge of the Grand Canyon, and she was talking about the colors, and said 'stupendous' and made rabbit ears for the ten zillionth time, and I just pushed her over the edge." "Case dismissed."

Carole tried not to watch the clock on her desk, which made her watch it. And then just as she was trying to decide how soon to leave the phone rang, and she debated rapidly, voted yes, and picked up the phone. It turned out to be a co-worker with a rather involved problem, so Carole said she had a luncheon appointment and promised to return the call soon after lunch.

She went to the ladies room, checked hair and makeup, and left the building. After a lot of thinking that morning she had chosen a modest suit with full skirt and jacket, a light peach color. All of that was on the outside, above the pounds and pounds of cement poured over the place where lay her broken heart and seethed her anger/love for Ken.

That morning she had brushed her teeth and chosen a suit to meet a man. It was the first time she had done that, chosen the right clothing for any man except Ken since he first said "I love you." Above the heavy cement, still wet in places, she chose the suit and went to work and on this date. Below was so much pain that it was too taxing, draining, frightening to deal with -- thus the cap, the seal of cement. Carole planned on getting some help, probably Dr. Ckeye whom she admired, but not just yet.

All day, somewhat over the past few days but especially today, a question kept bubbling up from the covered place -- "Why am I doing this?" As she walked towards the restaurant she answered it, spoke back to the question and said "Because someday I am going to have my first date, why not today!" Further than that, deeper experiences than lunch with a blind date, were for some other days. Perhaps those somedays included romance and love and marriage and sex -- or far more likely, she imagined, sex and marriage. In the divorced-persons-dating rule book, maybe the correct order was meet, date, sex, romance, marriage, love. Musing like that, she was suddenly at the restaurant. She stopped, startled a moment, and then went in.

Across the street, Ralph/Cary had watched an attractive lady in a light peach suit walking purposefully along, looking a bit grim with a set jaw, and decided that wasn't Carole since the woman looked like she would stride on by. Suddenly she stopped, as if coming out of a fog, her face softened, and she went into the restaurant. Ralph knew it was she, a lady carrying a lot of deadlove baggage, his blind date. He sighed, murmured to himself that this was a mistake, too soon for the lady with the baggage, and started to put down the book. Then he stopped, realized that he had really wanted to buy this novel -- a courtroom puzzler with good lawyers and bad, as in unlawful, lawyers and giant corporations and lots of money washing around – and he decided to purchase it. Fun to read, and talking about it and other books might be an ice-breaker. Worst case -- if the date fizzled he could read it for the rest of his lunch hour.

As Ralph stepped inside Bistro Roma to be struck instantly by the cool air and warm oregano and cheese aromas, the lady in peach was being shown to a table. He waited until she sat down, facing the door to watch for him as Ralph/Cary knew she would, and then as she looked up he raised a questioning hand, nodded towards her and mouthed "Carole?" She open her hands, good welcoming look on her face, and mouthed "Ralph?" End of Cary, but fun while it lasted.

He walked up to the table, and she held out her hand for a handshake, sparing him the decision. She had a firm grip, a businesswoman's handshake. They said hello, and then he sat down. The waiter came almost at once and said, seemingly in one breath "Hello my name is Lowell I'll be your waiter today may I take your drink order?"

Carole said "I will have ice tea. And separate checks, please."

The waiter, a very thin young man with black, straight hair and deep blue eyes, turned towards Ralph. "And you sir?" Ralph took him for a starving student or hungry actor.

"The same, thank you." Lowell flipped to the back of his order pad and, without looking at them said in the same hurried word stream, "We have three specials today monkfish on vermicelli with vegetable medley or pasta primavera or shrimp scampi the last two come with the house salad I'll be right back with your ice teas."

Ralph had set the book on the table, and Carole nodded towards it. "You like courtroom mysteries?"

"Yes, the intrigue and word games and brilliant thinking. The people in these books are always so fast on their feet. You know, real life, someone says something and the next day you come up with the perfect answer -- crush them with your wit, 24 hours late? Well, these people always have the crushing words right there, ready to say, perfect grammar and timing. Fun to read. You?"

"My job calls for so much reading, so much paper, or else I am crunching numbers. Paper and numbers all day. I pretty much read the newspaper and some magazines, but rarely a book. My treat is to read books on vacation -- have for years. Novels and mysteries, like that one," she said, indicating his book "a real pleasure. Only casual reading, escape into novels, not a financial document in sight." Inside her head visions of Ken and their last vacation flashed by. Jamie staying with her beloved aunt and uncle and cousins. Ken and Carole on the Carolina coast. Her reading exactly such an escape novel, sitting on the porch in that ankle-length white cotton skirt and halter top and he bringing her lemonade and that morning they had made love--.

Lowell came, left teas and disappeared in a flash, not ready to take their orders. Carole was relieved by the interruption, hoped that her face had not gone blank as Carolina memories rushed through her head. But Ralph had seen nothing, busy as he was working on a response to her reading choices, thinking "Don't let there be an awkward silence. Please let me make conversation with this woman."

Carole saved him from conversational pressure by picking up her menu. "Did you hear any of those specials that went flying by?"

"Yes, I'm thinking of the scampi, a little garlic butter might be just fine. And you?"

"Small Caesar salad, side-order of pasta with one meatball."

"Am I correct in guessing you have ordered that before?"

"Yes. Now you are getting a picture, aren't you, so early in this date. Accountant type, tons of paperwork, not well read, compulsively orders the same things."

Ralph laughed, liked her poking fun at herself. "Not at all, not at all. I admire and envy organization. Exploration does not always equal adventure, sometimes it equals chaos."

They chatted comfortably for a while, books and foods, something about their jobs. It was not hard for either of them, a fact he noticed and noted. As the moments passed, Ralph became aware that he was relaxing and enjoying himself. He knew she was divorced yet glanced, force of habit, at her left hand. The important finger was ringless, but the smooth and lighter skin color spoke of the wide band no longer there. Carole did no such reflecting. She was in another place, there on moon, talking to this nice man -- on a date! And all the time precious Jamie and Ken & Sukie and sex and the real world and the not-well-buried past swirled and stormed around her, bubbled up through the insecure cement cap. They were talking about their preferences in tea and coffee and, while the front of her brain carried on that conversation, she found herself remembering the time, long ago and soon after their marriage when they had dumped a whole pot of coffee on the bed. Carole and Ken having breakfast in bed on a Sunday morning, and then disaster. The only thing to do with the coffee soaked mattress was to take it outside, there in the apartment complex courtyard, and let it dry in the warm sun while neighbors guessed about the large dark stain in the middle of the newlyweds' mattress.

Lowell showed up, not knowing that he had rescued her. It was a strain to keep making pleasant, neutral small talk. It was fine meeting Tom's friend Ralph and talking to him. Just fine. But the memories flashed and crowded most annoyingly. Not with every word spoken or every concept, but there were trip wires everywhere, unknowable until one tripped and, while talking of books or coffee, suffered a flash of Carolina or a special Sunday morning. He took their orders on separate checks, glanced at their half-full ice tea glasses, said "Let me put your orders in and get you some more tea" and then he left.

Carole wasn't sure why memories were popping up at this particular, terribly inappropriate moment, this lunch date. At work, and most of the day, the cement cap stayed on fairly tight, only the occasional bubble from below. At night of course there were occasional problems, but she had taken to a combination of reading and soft music. The reading, as she had told Ralph, was very hard to do at the end of the day; difficult to keep her eyes open, reading in bed on a comfortable pillow. Fifteen minutes, sometimes less. What she didn't say was that was exactly the intended effect. At first the music was an annoyance, and she couldn't drift off with it playing, but that soon changed, and now she was put to sleep by the masters: Brahms, Tchaikovsky, Beethoven. She woke in the middle of the night, the format having switched to jazz or blues, listened a while and then turned it off. She was relearning how to sleep well while sleeping alone.

"Oh what the hell," Carole said inside her head. Enough of the light chat, maybe something more substantive would quiet the annoying demons for a while. "Ralph, you know I am very recently divorced."

"Yes."

"Did you know you are my first -- this is my first date?"

"No, Tom didn't say that, just -- uh, ah -- that he liked you and that he thought we would have, be -- he thought we should meet." Ralph finished in a bit of a rush.

"Ralph, you didn't pause and say 'uh, ah' when we were talking about reading materials. What did my dear Tom really say?"

"Must I?"

"Sure. If I'm going to start dating I need to know how all

this works."

"Let me say that it was mythology about recently divorced ladies."

Carole smiled. "OK, I'll quit with that. So what is it like, this adult dating thing?"

"Got me! This is my first date in years."

She laughed, and it felt good. Lowell showed up, nice timing, and put their plates in front of them. The scampi was sizzling hot, the salad crisp, the one meatball firm and flavorful with not too much sauce on properly cooked pasta. They both ate a few bites, agreed that it was quite tasty, and ate some more. Then Ralph sat back.

"So you want to know about adult dating. Well, what do you want first, the good news or the bad news?"

"I have a friend, a woman. Her good news bad news was that sometimes people connect, but there are lots of dead ends. 'Single world abounds with dead ends' was her phrase. So the good first, to give me strength. Then I'll decide if I can hear bad, or sad."

"Well, OK, the good news. The good news -- gee, the bad news is so much easier to do -- are you sure I can't start there?"

She laughed "Your choice."

He noticed that she cut her pasta with the edge of her fork and conveyed it easily, without a slip. "One of the dating things goes all the way back to high school, and that is the list of things to never order while on a date."

"Which are?"

"Spaghetti, for sure. Dropping it in your lap and making slurping sounds and red sauce on your clean shirt -- none of which you are doing, he hastened to add." Again, her easy laugh. He liked it. "I must say I am dazzled by your smooth handling. Can you also do the spoon-twirl thing?"

"Yes, but I would rather cut it, although I know purists would not approve. Had many a serving of pasta over the years. We are good friends. So what else is on the high school do-not-order-on-a-date list?"

"High school and beyond. Let's see -- fried chicken, or anything else greasy or usually eaten with fingers. French onion soup with the melted cheese on top. That long string of cheese from the bowl to your mouth, so very suave. Probably any soup is a potential danger. Sandwiches are OK, except things like chicken salad that falls on your plate or into your water glass."

Carole was enjoying herself. This relaxed, pleasant man was good company. She realized that the conversation had drifted away from the subject of adult dating but didn't feel like pursuing it. It was just nice to be here, the memory flashes had subsided. It had become just a good lunch with good conversation. A good time.

An hour had passed, the dishes were cleared, the separate checks presented and checks with credit cards collected by fast-moving Lowell. Ralph looked at her and said "I like you and your laugh. And your ability to neatly consume spaghetti with sauce. May I see you again?"

Carole sat there, hesitated a moment too long.

Before she could respond he said, not unkindly and with a slight smile, "Well, that was a warm reception! Was it the garlic on the scampi?"

Now she smiled, shook her head slightly. "No, I like being with you and with the garlic. I had some too, the salad was loaded! It's just, just that I just -- do I keep saying 'just'? Please, another try. I am very recently divorced. I have a daughter who is dealing with it, and although her father and I have been apart almost a year I'm certain she thought we might -- fix it. Get back together. So my dating means moving on from her father, and this will not be easy for her -- not as hard to accept as the split, but another step to take. And then there is me. I have -- I'm not ready for you to like me." Carole's eyes widened. What a personal comment to this stranger! Ralph made a little "That's OK" gesture, tilting his head and opening both hands, palms down. He said nothing. Before an uncomfortable moment could build Lowell showed up once again with prescient timing, deposited the credit cards and the credit slips with room for tipping and signing. He thanked them and invited them to please come again, quite unaware that his automatic parting words had real significance to these two people and the conversation, the silence, he had interrupted.

Ralph and Carole computed the tips, added them and signed their names. They rose at the same time, giving him no chance to pull out her chair. She held out her hand, again gave him that solid, professional handshake, and said "It was a pleasure meeting you. I mean that. I'm not ready -- but thank you."

"I do believe I'm going to call you again."

She replied, gently and with a slight smile, "Goodbye, Ralph" and left. He looked at her a moment, remembered his book and turned back to get it. She was gone.

Almost as soon as Carole was back in her office after lunch, Tom was there, almost bouncing from eagerness.

"Relax, Tom, you did good. A fine fix-up."

"You guys set the date?"

"Not quite. Actually, eager cupid, I don't think I'm ready for dating. Thought I might be, but maybe a little more time before I can do that."

"You didn't like him."

"I did like him, really. Thomas, I don't want to talk about my emotions now. Just accept that you did a good job; he is a nice man and I'm not ready to date."

"And you will have to accept that I'm going to try again. I think you'd be so cool together, my office buddy and my golfing buddy."

"That's another thing. He is more than your golfing buddy, he is your teenage buddy. Early teenage. You didn't tell me you were in high school together."

"So? He did graduate, I swear."

"You are three years younger than I am, which makes him

three years younger. I guess it isn't a problem, but Ken is two years older than me, so it was quite a contrast. A surprise."

"You are a sexist! No, an -- an ageist!"

"No I'm not. It wasn't a negative, just an observation."

"Shall I make an observation about the advantages of younger men?"

"For older women? Excuse me, I have to go get my hair tinted blue. And you have to return to your desk, don't you?"

"Sure, got to call Ralph, ask him what he thought of you and your blue hair. Any message?"

A sad smile. "No message."

Tom did as he promised, called Ralph as soon as he got back to his desk. "Well, numbnuts, you weren't gone very long. You a lousy date? Do I have to apologize for you?"

"See, the thing is, we've been friends so long I know instantly when you are bullshitting."

"Such as?"

"We were at the restaurant almost an hour, and I'm sure you know that, probably put the stopwatch on her when she walked out the door. Also, since she has been back for a while, you were either working or talking to her about our lunch. I'll sell you my new putter for a dollar if you were working."

"Ha! The putter is mine!"

"Really?"

"No, can't steal from a friend. Anyway that putter isn't worth a dollar."

"It's a fine putter. I was just off my game, that's all."

"Implying you have game to be on."

"So when you talked to her you found out I was not a lousy date, didn't blow my nose on the tablecloth once."

"You liked her, right? Neat lady, cute, like I said."

"Down boy, down. She said she isn't ready to date. That's what she said, not ready. Now that could mean that she thinks I'm bat-shit ugly and was being kind--"

"You are, but some dames like you bat-shit guys."

"Dames. I don't know anyone but you who says that any-more."

"'There Is Nothing Like A Dame.' Great song, one of my favorites. Sing it in the shower all the time."

"And Gracie still loves you. Amazing. As I was saying. I don't think it was my looks or table manners. I think she meant it. She seemed to be wound pretty tight. Don't think she's near over him."

"I consider this only the slightest of setbacks. You'll see, you two are going to connect."

"Connect this. Want a golf lesson Sunday?"

"From the man who three putts from three feet? Wish I could, but we are doing the in-law thing this weekend. May-be next week."

"Call me."

Chapter Twenty

As Trudy drove into the busy parking lot and slowed almost to a stop to look for a space, Carole studied those going in and out of the Rockery. It was a cool, beautiful evening. Some people lingered near the doorway but most were going in, few out. "Going to be packed tonight," Trudy said, sticking the nose of her car into a space just as the previous occupant pulled out, nearly scraping fenders but winning the parking game. "Hope you wore your best deodorant!"

Carole didn't respond. She was trying to guess the age and maturity level of those heading toward the Rockery through the brightly lit parking lot. Almost all were clearly younger, in their early twenties, eight to ten years from her. Some, though, appeared to be thirties and some forties and a few beyond that. A mixed group, drawn by the mix of classic album and top forty rock. The Rockery was a fairly large building that had gone through several iterations as restaurants and nightclubs. Now it pumped out music with the unloseable back beat, solid 4/4, good old rock and roll. There was a ring of neon circles around the word "Rockery," also in neon. All were brightly lit and in good working order, attracting and welcoming and garish at the same time.

Carole braced for the assault of loud music, but the owners wanted their place to be a popular date spot and singles meet market, so the volume, while loud, was moderated enough that conversation, spoken loudly but still conversation, was possible. There was some tobacco smoke but not a stinging amount. The number of smokers was only about a fourth of those present, and the filters and electric precipitators removed much of what those puffing produced.

Beer was everywhere. Some men held glasses but the majority drank from bottles. The women reversed the percents, very few women drinking from bottles. Empty beer bottles sat on tables or were propped on chair rails around the walls. A few people, mostly women, mostly over 30, ordered mixed drinks. All beverages, and the free, salty/spicy mix that made you need another drink, were delivered by the hard working, fast moving female wait staff, all dressed in sturdy running shoes, jean cutoffs and Rockery T-shirts accented by uplift bras. Somehow they managed to keep the orders straight, clean up abandoned tables with spilled beer and bottles and glasses -- some with drowned cigarettes -- make change or take and return credit cards, smile and keep moving fast and respond promptly enough to earn good tips. All this in addition to the challenge of carrying full trays through crowds of people starting and stopping and changing direction in their pursuit of mates, or dates, or scores. The seekers barely noticed the waitresses avoiding collisions with almost every step.

Trudy spotted her three friends from work. Carole was introduced to them by a nearly-shouting Trudy, and Carole said hello, making little attempt to grab the names. Like Trudy, they had the ease and somewhat edgy extraversion of regulars. They were sitting on bar stools clustered at a high small round table with just enough room for their drinks and two ashtrays, one in use. The women swiveled on their stools to turn and respond to a touch on the shoulder or loud-enough voice or just to people-watch. From time to time a man would stop by, sometimes chat a moment or suggest a dance. The women always said yes. Since Carole did not know them, the women or men, she was left out of this. Trudy kept trying to bring her into the circle, and Carole would join for a while to share a joke, but it was fine with her to just sip her vodka lemonade and watch. She enjoyed the multi-directional parade, the constant and constantly changing spontaneous floor show, the flirting and posing and rock dancing. Fun to watch.

The dance floor was down a step from the rest of the room. It was surrounded by a sturdy rail on which leaned mostly men, some women, almost all with drink in hand. Empty bottles were left here and there on the rail, removed by the non-stop troops in jean cutoffs and pointing T-shirts who also took and delivered orders to the rail crowd. Some on the rail were alone, others in pairs or small groups. Most watched the dancers who displayed a wide range of talent, including some on the lower end of that range. Those dancers, all male, sort of hopped from one foot to the other, sort of in time to the beat while the female he was dancing with got it right.

A few of those at the rail leaned against it, their backs to the dancers watching the tables, scanning the room and the entrance from the lobby where one paid the cover charge at the door and used the long, narrow, crowded coatroom or bought cigarettes or used the two stark white restrooms. At the tables, watched by the rail-leaners facing their way, were groups of women and groups of men -- males the majority under thirty, females over thirty -- talking and drinking and flirting and occasionally heading towards the dance floor. Once in a rare while two women danced, never two men.

Carole noticed one man leaning with his back to the rail. He had dark curly hair, long in back, thinning in front. His silk, patterned shirt was open a careful three buttons -- collar and two more -- revealing his curly chest hair and the double loops of a flat gold chain. His very fashionable dark blue jeans were too tight. He seemed to have stepped right out of a bad independent movie about life in the fast lane, a living stereotype.

Out on the dance floor one man and his partner were taking up a lot of real estate, and everyone let them. He was an excellent dancer, by far the best in the room. He held his partner's hand, spun and twirled her, spun himself and met up with her in perfect synchronization like a majorette throwing and catching a spinning baton without missing a beat. He was smooth, creative, and totally disconnected from his partner. He held her hand, touched her back or hip as she spun by, guided her flawlessly but never looked at her, never smiled or made an attempt to meet her eyes. His gaze, somewhat vacant, was wherever his head was pointed; since he usually had his head tilted to his left that's where his eyes were aimed, but it was clear he could have done about as well blindfolded. Her purpose was to dance with him. He couldn't do all those spins and passes unless he had someone, some woman, to spin and pass. It didn't matter who she was, as long as she could keep up and do the steps. It also didn't matter to his partner that he was so distant. Women who were sick of dancing with men who hopped to the beat of a different drummer, or women who were sick of sitting, or women who could really dance and wanted to do all those pass-twirl-spin steps in fine style, would approach him with a word, "Dance?" Or sometimes a pointing hand would invite him to share some Pointer Sisters or Elvis or Stones or Aretha or Bobby Darin or ZZ Top or Zeppelin; a wide mixture for the fairly wide range of ages and tastes of the patrons. He, the dancing man, would agree without gesture but just by heading towards the floor with her, and they would dance. Then he would say "Thanks," that's all he ever said, "Thanks." Sometimes he would take a short break, but the dancing man was there to dance -- all alone while holding the hands of numerous partners, hours a night.

One of Trudy's male co-workers stopped by and she shouted introductions to Carole. He said hello with a quick handshake, then took Trudy to the dance floor. She danced two numbers with him, recent rock by a teenage boys group followed by the Righteous Brothers' Unchained Melody to allow the slow dancers a turn. Trudy and her pal from work laughed and talked through the song, she cueing the cymbal crash. No hint of romance, just buddies. As they parted at the end of the song, she turned and found herself facing the dancing man just as he delivered "Thanks" to his departing partner. She reached out a hand and he took it as the next rock tune cranked up, enough of that slow stuff. They danced well together.

Comfortable on her bar stool, Carole watched her friend. No one had approached her to dance, but this evening was for enjoyment and escape and to please Trudy, no need to connect with men. She watched Trudy and the dancing man, and then followed Trudy with her eyes as she worked her way back to the table. The path she had chosen took her directly past the man with the curly chest and the flattened gold. The aisle was crowded, and Trudy found herself passing closely to and half facing him. She turned her head toward him and said "Hi!" He responded by staring oh so sexy into her eyes and giving her a small, slow, regal nod. She kept going.

Trudy's friend, Phil Peterson, returned and asked her to dance again but she insisted he ask Carole, and it was fine. He was a good dancer and escorted her to and from the table. They stayed another half-hour, then headed home. When Carole got out she realized that she had not left any lights on, Jamie staying at the Jensen's. The dark house looked strange. Trudy waited until Carole opened her door and waived before turning into her own driveway and hitting the garage door remote.

Carole turned on some lights and started to get ready for bed, aware as she stripped that her clothes smelled of cigarette smoke. She started to get into bed but the smell was strong on her hair and arms. "Too stinky to sleep with" she said, showered quickly, and soon was asleep.

Chapter Twenty-One

Ralph waited two weeks before calling Carole.

"Carole Tagee, Financial Services."

"Hello, Carole, Ralph Donnell. How are you?"

"Fine Ralph, and you?"

"Doing fine, thanks. As promised, I'm calling. The Deep Cove Dinner Theatre is doing Guys and Dolls. You know, 'Luck be a Lady Tonight,' 'I'll Know.' Great stuff. And stuffing. With turkey and gravy. Week from Saturday?"

The slightest hesitation. "I'm sorry. I need to spend more time with Jamie. My daughter."

"Yes."

"I promised her we would go to a movie."

A beat.

"Well, OK."

Another beat.

"Thanks for asking."

"Sure. Goodbye."

"Goodbye."

Not knowing about the phone call, Tom and Gracie assumed their help was needed to move the matchmaking along. Tom knew Ralph since high school, worked with Carole many years, and had an unwavering conviction that the two belonged together. Goodness of fit he called it. Gracie had met Carole, knew Ralph through the men's friendship. Ralph had been one of the ushers at their wedding, and he sometimes visited before or after the golf outing, shared a few double dates and holidays.

Tom and Gracie Lagrinka had been married five years. Gracie had suffered ovarian cysts as a teenager and knew before she married that she couldn't have children. When Tom proposed she told him yes if he wanted her in her condition. He responded "'A-ly I love you, B-ly we won't need rubbers or pills, and C-ly someday we'll adopt." And so they were married. Shortly after their fourth anniversary they both felt it was time to begin the adoption procedure. It wasn't one convincing the other, but rather both knowing the time had come.

As a first step they began looking for a house. The luxury apartment complex they lived in was great for singles or childless couples, complete with party room and pool. But impending parenthood necessitated a single-family dwelling, a fenced backyard, room to play with baby Lagrinka. And room to teach the baby the fundamentals of a good golf swing, lessons to begin a week or two after baby's first steps were taken. Tom and Gracie had the comic patter well-rehearsed.

"Probably the same day" said Gracie. "I can see it now. She stands up, takes two steps, and Tom starts teaching her the overlapping grip."

"And taking her - or him, maybe him - out back to the putting green I have cleverly built."

"Garden comes first. Putting green if there's room."

With the searches for a house and a child well under way, the Lagrinkas decided to reserve the pool and party room for a Saturday evening. As soon as they decided to have the party they called or asked everyone to make sure lots of friends could attend. The mailed invitations were reminders, and an excuse to exercise their wit:

We are giving up a fine apartment, where someone else fixes things, for a house where we do all the work. We are giving up a swimming pool, and instead will have grass to mow. We are making this move so we can give up our freedom and stay home with a baby. Best of all, we get our baby not the usual fun way but by doing paperwork and spending money. Come celebrate our insanity at a poolside party. Who knows if there will ever be another.

Matchmaking was therefore not the primary purpose for the party, but it was a great opportunity. And so, several weeks after the declined invitation to the dinner theatre, Ralph and Carole were each invited to the pool party. They had no choice but to attend.

Going to a pool party can have great significance to a couple even if they have had only one date. It is a leap towards intimacy or away from it, a preview of what might be in store should friendship become romance, and while personal parts are covered it doesn't take a lot of imagination to picture the other nude. Bellies, thighs, chests and breasts are exposed or indicated with only a slight distortion of the truth. Scar on your shoulder, beauty mark on your inner thigh? Now she will know, he will know. Look and know before touching.

Tom and Ralph sat talking on one side of the pool while Carole and Gracie sat on the other, a neighbor between them. The neighbor was a rather striking woman with reddish hair and freckles on her face and neck and down onto what was exposed of her splendid breasts by her bikini top.

"Ah, Ralph me lad, tis a fine sight to behold."

"You're as Irish as a kielbasa, Grinks. But tell me, Irish Thomas O'Lagrinka, are ye speakin'o' yer fine wife? Or Lady Carole is it? Or could it be lustful thinkin' about the redheaded lassie?"

"Know what I always wonder?" Tom said, the accent gone.

"Of course I know I know what you always wonder. We've been friends since far too long, fist fuck."

"All right, numbnuts, what?"

Ralph sighed wearily. "You are wondering how far down the freckles go."

"Yes. Are they freckled to the nip?"

"Ask her. Walk over there, say you are sorry to interrupt but your penis-led brain needs to know something, and just ask her. I think she's proud of them, maybe she'll show you."

"Better yet, I'll invite her for a swim, and accidentally get my hand caught in her top. Her tit in my mouth."

"My dick in your ear. I'm going swimming."

Ralph stood up, took off his shirt and dove in the pool. Tom followed, and they splashed around a few minutes then swam over to the other side, the deep end, where they hung on the edge.

"Can the gab. Get in the water" Tom shouted.

"This is the man I want to raise my child" Gracie said to the other women. To Tom "Try again, dear."

"Fine and gracious ladies, please join us for a dip in the pool. In return we will not only soonly grill you burgers and the dogs known as hot but serve them to you on plates of the finest paper. And with beverages."

"Much better" said Gracie.

"If I swim with you you'll serve me dinner? That'll work." The bikini with freckles walked right to the edge, Tom and Ralph gazing upward at the sight, then she laughed and dove over their heads.

"Thomas, the last time I saw you that slack-jawed was on our wedding night. You are such a bad influence on Ralph. Ralph, return your pupils to normal, Tom close your mouth, and then Carole and I will join you. If you still want us to, that is."

"Please" said Tom."

"Yes please" said Ralph.

So there the two men were, hanging on the edge of the pool, bare shoulders and chests, looking up at the two women. When Carole stood she was painfully aware of her body.

She took off her matching jacket and dropped it on the chair. She hesitated a brief moment and Ralph got it. He pushed away, turned, dove under. When he came up she was just entering the water in a dive, Gracie easing in off a ladder. The four met, then swam to the five-foot section. Freckles was poised and posing on the diving board. The four swam to the shallower water and were soon joined by several others.

Tom turned towards Carole. "I think it would be the polite and proper thing for me to greet our guests by name. Who is that very unattractive woman you were talking to, poor child that she is?"

"Why, how kind of you, Tom! Yes, a sad case of a woman with more curves than the suit can cover."

"I didn't notice."

Carole laughed and splashed Tom with several handfuls of water. Ralph, standing near while in a discussion of the upcoming pro football season, turned his head at the sound of her laughter. More of the guests joined them, a party in the five-foot section of the pool. Conversations, kidding, splashing, people swimming short distances and back. Gracie turned to respond to a greeting from a friend, Tom left to follow the freckles off the diving board, then Ralph turned and found himself close to Carole, the two alone surrounded by the splashing, laughing crowd, in water to their chests.

"How was the movie?"

Carole blinked. "Oh. Fine, thanks. I'm always pleased when Jamie and I can find a movie we both like. She's too old for 'Sleeping Beauty' and too young for almost everything else."

Ralph pushed a small wave with his hands. "What did you see?"

"Do you know the Birch's theater? Lots of classics for a low price. Two Bugs Bunny cartoons and Rear Window for three-fifty a ticket."

"Jamie hadn't seen it before."

"No, in fact those actors mean nothing to her. It was fun

to share."

A pause, filled by entertainment from the deep end. Tom roared as he tucked his knees and delivered a monstrous cannonball, the diving board bouncing behind him.

"The dinner theater was good" he said without her asking. "What a corny plot, what great song and dance numbers. 'Fugue for Tinhorns, Got the horse right here.' Great."

Beat.

"Should I try again?"

"Ralph, I'm not ready. Just not ready."

"Ready for what? I offered dinner, not a diamond. Look, I don't pressure ladies. I like you, but if you want to pass there's no problem. I have to get Tom away from that bikini and busy on the grill or we'll all starve. Take care, Carole. Good seeing you."

He ducked down, turned under water and swam towards the cannonballer.

The grill was natural gas with lava rocks, so the cooking could soon begin. Veggies and dips were almost gone; time for some serious food. While Tom, Ralph and a few other men did the guy thing at the grill with the fire and meat, Carole and Gracie got out and toweled off, then went into the party house.

Some of the women had gone off the diving board or allowed their hair to get thoroughly wet while swimming, but most had not. Gracie's hair was only a bit wet from Tom's splashing, but Carole with her short wash and wear hair had not been concerned, and even swam a few laps. In the party house she showered, put on panties and bra, used her crystal deodorant stick and dressed in half-hose, khaki slacks and loafers. A blue blouse would be added as soon as her hair was done.

The ladies' room was well supplied with small hair dryers, hair spray, nail files, spray deodorant. Side by side the two women made reflected eye contact.

"So, what do you think?"

"You talk like your husband; I'm supposed to guess about what. OK, I guess about Ralph. What do I think about Ralph."

"Rather I didn't ask? 'Still too early to decide' won't offend me."

"I like him. I like talking to him."

"Friendly."

"However---"

"Not friendly. No, go ahead" Gracie said with a laugh.

"I'm still sorting me out. It doesn't make sense that I, or anyone divorced, starts looking as soon as the papers are signed. You know, walk out of the courthouse looking for love. Except those people who already have a new love." Carole held a dryer, low heat, while fluffing her hair, shaking her head with her chin held up. Over the sound of the dryer's motor she said "So let's say there is love for the divorced. If I, or we, don't start looking as the ink dries on the divorce degree, then we start -- someday. When is someday, Gracie? When do I want to kiss another, bed another?"

Carole shut off the dryer and looked at Gracie through their reflections in the mirror, looked hard, almost defiantly.

Softer. "I'm not pushing, Carole."

Carole turned and faced Gracie. She put out a hand and stroked Gracie's shoulder with a 'That's all right' gesture. "Tom is," she said with a sad smile.

"He likes you both very much. He sees you together. Those two have been friends a long time, and brothers couldn't be closer. He doesn't want his buddy to be alone."

Several women came spilling into the room, talking and laughing. The spell broken, Gracie and Carole finished dressing and went to find the food.

Some of the men had dressed, but most were still in their swimsuits with loafers or other footwear and a shirt added, occasionally topped off by a hat. The party became food, drink, and lively conversation. Tom, assisted by Ralph and a few other men, was wreathed in smoke, dispensing hamburgers, hot dogs and Polish sausage. "Burgers! Who wants a rare one? Got a burnt dog here!"

Carole sat near Gracie, was hungry and concentrated on her food. She had selected a slightly burnt kielbasa and topped it with spicy mustard and chopped onions. She also got potato salad, cole slaw, and a lemonade spiked with rum.

While eating Carole watched the people settle down. They paired off, and it was suddenly quite clear that there were five single, or unpaired, people. The males were Ralph and another man in his early sixties, a charming retired fireman. Carole had talked to him briefly and told him about her father's nickname. The unpaired females were Carole, the freckled redhead and a blond woman who Carole guessed was about her age or a little older. Everyone else was with someone, and they ate together, got each other something to drink, offered bites of their sandwiches.

Tom came to where they were sitting and offered a bowl of Cajun-spiced potato chips, a bag he had forgotten to open and now was in a hurry to share. Both women took a few. Tom turned away, then back with great drama. "By the way, Gracie, I want you to know that even though you have almost no freckles I love you very much and can hardly wait to have your baby." He spun away to offer the chips to others, leaving Gracie smiling and Carole aching a little.

A lively discussion was starting, the ageless "what is wrong with the opposite sex." Most of the crowd joined in, moving their chairs to form a rough circle. Women and men bandied about such pedestrian complaints as stinky sneakers, panty hose drying in the bathroom, a true talent for embarrassing noises, long hair in the bathroom sink trap, too much air conditioning in the summer, too much heat in the winter. People howled with laughter, made revealing statements they surely would hear about later. Then the single blond spoke up.

"I like men a lot, despite their many faults. But what really gets me is that so many of them have no idea what great sex is."

This sparked a series of high school humor about body shapes and sizes, staying power, and more personal comments and revelations. Laughter on laughter, a howling good time, but clearly the couples were enjoying and connecting to the discussion and jokes at a different, far more intimate level than those without a partner.

Ralph spoke up, looking at the blond. "OK, for those of us who are not four-star experts, I would like to hear your opinion on what great sex is. I myself, of course, have a three and three-quarters star rating" -- this to general laughter and a "taught the boy all I know!" comment from Tom, earning him a swift rib dig from Gracie -- "but I am open to suggestions. Pray tell, what is great sex?"

The woman gave him a smile, then looked down at the glass in her hand. She turned it and turned it as she spoke, looking at the glass, spoke as if remembering. "This is great sex. First, you get all dressed up and go someplace wonderful. Dinner at a special restaurant. Or a play or musical or opera. Something emotional like "La Bohème." Or maybe a restaurant and a movie. But you don't want to be too tired.

"Main-TAIN that stamina!" said one of the men.

She continued, still talking to the glass. "Then you come back, get in bed, hold each other close, kiss a little, start getting a little hot, and go to sleep."

This last caught everyone by surprise so much that there were no immediate comments. She continued.

"The next morning you have your favorite breakfast -- got to make sure you have everything you need, do the shopping the day before. Then you sit a while, read, listen to some good music. Classics -- Mozart, Vivaldi, the real stuff. Be quiet together till breakfast has a chance to settle. Fill the tub, take a bath, wash each other nice and clean. By now you should both be feeling a little crazy. And then you go to bed and just -- just be real good to each other." She looked up, her eyes a little moist. "And that, friends and neighbors, is great sex."

The party changed after that, became quieter, more intimate. The blond soon left, perhaps feeling she had revealed too much, or perhaps a memory stung. Carole felt as if her singleness was a neon sign for all to see. Ralph felt sad.

The evening passed. A few men went back in, but only one woman, the lady endowed with the fabulous freckles. People were leaving, saying goodbye and wishing Tom and Gracie the best of luck with their pending new responsibilities. Ralph began helping with the clean up as did Carole, and they found themselves, the four, busy cleaning. As they worked, Gracie caught Tom's eye and with raised eyebrows and tiny head nod indicated Ralph and Carole -- "look who is still here" said her glances. But nothing romantic happened. When the work ended, Tom and Ralph were near the gate, the women near the party house. Ralph turned and called a goodbye to Gracie and Carole. They both called goodnight to him, and he was gone. Gracie looked at Carole. Carole shrugged sadly.

Chapter Twenty-Two

As on Carole's first visit, Dr. Ckeye came out of her office to welcome her. She was dressed in a soft, A-line dress of forest green, gown and hair and faint makeup perfect.

"Good to see you, Carole. Please come in."

Carole took the same chair she had last time. "Thank you for seeing me so quickly. I have been thinking about you, about coming to see you, well, actually since the day I was here."

"Has something happened?"

"I'm getting a little tired of me. No, a lot tired -- tired of being weepy, tired of thinking about Ken. I met a nice man, got fixed up actually, but I just couldn't think about, couldn't focus on him. I don't know. He may be gone."

"A telephone call is one way to find out. Or a letter, a good old-fashioned letter. If you are ready to focus, that is. I may be presuming something that hasn't happened."

"My being ready to focus on a new man, a new partner?"

"Yes. How do you feel about that?"

"Well I'm not kidding myself. I've read the articles, talked to women, had several conversations with a friend about my age who has been looking hard for some time. I'm in my mid-thirties, a teenager at home. As I understand it, my chances of finding a suitable partner are something like being struck by lightning or winning the lottery."

"Perhaps not quite so unlikely."

"Perhaps. But I'm not concentrating on that, the man search. I do want to see some new faces and hear new ideas. I'm ready to open up, invite new people into my life. So I invite and mingle, date, and that may lead to a relationship. Maybe not. As for a permanent relationship--" Carole shrugged.

"Ready to explore."

"Let it happen. As my daughter and her friends say, whatever. Never quite get the inflection right, have to say it through the nose. What-ev-er."

They both sat quietly for a few moments.

"I do want a person, a companion, if I can find him. I feel it's time. Time for exploring, dating, mingling, with luck finding. I've been thinking about coming to see you with the idea that this visit is a turning point. It's where I start down a new road."

"Perhaps you have already begun that journey."

"Perhaps. I am still wrestling with confusion, separating the loss from the humiliation and rejection."

"Please say some more, talk about those words -- loss, humiliation, rejection."

"Part is the grieving, I understand that. I loved him. Only recently have I been saying that past tense, and I'm not sure if it is completely true. I feel like he will always have a piece of my heart."

Dr. Ckeye leaned forward, looking at Carole with her bright turquoise eyes. "Do you believe there must be no vestiges of love left? That if he does always stay with you in some corner of your heart you are then blocked from loving another?"

"No, but I thought he would go away, and he hasn't."

"And he may never. You lived with him and loved him for almost a decade and a half. You have a child together. Those things are true, and if your heart wants to give them their due isn't that understandable?"

"That was then, this is now, that's a memory."

"Yes. 'I will never forget you' doesn't have to mean 'I can never love another.' Widows, especially young war widows, have carried memories into new loves, done so for eons."

"But that is different -- actually, that brings me to the next word you wanted me to talk about. Humiliation. He didn't die, he left me. Dumped. I feel humiliated. Well, felt is more accurate, I guess. I don't really feel humiliated anymore."

"Why did you ever?"

"Because I was dumped. Viewed as not worth keeping. Out with the trash."

"Not really."

"No, not really." Carole sighed, turned in her chair and picked up the silver carafe, offered to fill Dr. Ckeye's glass.

"Thank you, yes." Carole filled both glasses, put the carafe down on its coaster, the stopper back in. She held her glass in her lap.

"But still it was a marriage failure, and a rejection, my ego flat as a pancake. And I miss Ken. Miss the love, companionship, counting on him. That reliable, trustworthy husband of mine. Which brings me to another problem, my naiveté. Foolish me. So I think I have been having problems separating them, unmixing the loss and the missing him from the embarrassment of being a castoff, a reject, and all the questions about why I didn't spot the evasions, the lying."

"If one is trusting, not looking, it is not easy, or natural, to pick up on this or that event and conclude that one's spouse is untrue. Strong marriages are built on trust. Certainly we all know that. If the marriage is strong, feels good and positive, then there seems to be no place for deceit. So many times I've heard men and women say 'How could my partner do this to me? I didn't suspect a thing.' They didn't suspect -- you didn't, because your marriage felt strong. Am I sounding too circular?"

"No, that makes a lot of sense. You either live in a state of doubt or a state of trust, and people in a state of trust occasionally get blindsided."

"Exactly. If you are living in a state of trust you aren't looking for -- and likely may miss -- terrible clues. Being unaware is the price paid on occasion by those who love and trust. It is also the assumption that the other person is abiding by the contract as you are."

"Marriage vows?"

"Yes, but I'm not using the word contract to mean only a legal marriage. Two people who are committed, who promise to have sex only with each other, have made a pact, a contract. Like this: if I'm not in any way considering another, and we're happy, then I can't imagine my partner is considering breaking, or has broken, the contract. How could I know if it never entered my mind to even suspect?"

Carole nodded. "Those are precious words. Thank you."

"As to the mixing of emotions, your words tell me that you are now doing a better job of making those separations. Do you agree?"

"Yes, and that is making things easier. But I am still angry with him, still hurt. He took another woman into our bed! I don't think I can ever forgive him."

"Why is it important that you forgive him?"

Carole started to answer then paused, started again. "I thought I couldn't go on, heal up -- I thought I couldn't be with someone else as long as I am still mad at him."

"I certainly agree with that. Let me give you a way of thinking about our mental processes, our daily emotions and thoughts. I believe that in any day we have a certain amount of psychic energy, mental gasoline in the tank. We can use it up thinking, planning, loving, hating, but at the end of the day we are empty, done. It isn't just our bodies that need rest, certainly our minds do too. 'Too tired to think' is a description of something we have all felt, and it doesn't mean our joints or muscles. Carole, every day you, all of us, burn up our tank full of psychic energy. I don't see you steeped in hate, not at all, thank goodness. But too often I do see people in this office who are consumed, who think they can never forgive, never let go of their anger."

"And you say --?"

"I ask how they feel about burning their daily tank full of energy on anger rather than on themselves. I urge them to consider how much better it is to spend it learning how to love another or to paint or play a musical instrument or speak another language or volunteer in a homeless shelter. Spend that psychic energy on yourself or on those in need -- not on one who is gone and not returning."

"Do they listen?"

"Eventually, almost everyone I meet with. The problem is, with some people 'eventually' is a long, long time. So maybe you shouldn't concentrate on forgiving or not forgiving, but rather on letting go. Let it go, let the anger go."

"I think I am there. Almost."

"Try to describe where you are now."

"With--?"

"The loss."

"He is gone. Husband Ken is now my ex. If I want love I need to find someone else, because it won't be Ken. So I guess I have accepted the loss."

"Humiliation and rejection?"

"I spent a long time not hearing, not accepting his 'It's not you, it's me.' He changed, went away from me emotionally. He broke the bond because he wasn't the man I married. It doesn't make me happy, but I am getting there, getting to the concept that this is about Ken's evolution, or devolution, not Carole's shortcomings."

"That sounds like humiliation and rejection are fading, victims to logic and acceptance. Good for you."

Carole smiled. "Yes, good for me."

"How is Jamie doing? How is her relationship with you and with Ken?"

"You anticipated me. I wanted to ask you how worried I should be."

Again Dr. Ckeye leaned forward, her hands folded in her lap, a look of concern on her face. "What is happening that worries you?"

"This sounds like a punch line, but I really don't know what to think. The answer is nothing, nothing is happening. Jamie acts as if her parents have been separated since birth, as if it has always been like this. She spends time with him, with me, and although sometimes she aggravates me, and her father, I know it is nothing compared to what some parents go through. Actually I hear stories from my married friends about their kids and I think either we did something very right or we sure are lucky."

"So you're worried because you see no symptoms."

"Looking for trouble, am I? Maybe I should just thank the stars for an understanding daughter."

"Have you or Ken, if you know, asked her how she is doing with the divorce, the two households?"

"Sort of. I don't know about Ken. Don't debrief James--"

"James?"

"Jamie Sue. Nickname since early childhood. I use it more than Ken. I asked her once if she would like us to stop, not call her by a boy's name, but she said she likes it, pictures it spelled with a final z."

Dr. Ckeye smiled broadly. "Wonderful. You were saying about debriefing--"

"I never ask about conversations. I'll ask if she had a good time, formula question, and she usually wants to tell me. They go see a movie, or stay at his apartment where she does homework, then they watch TV or play board games or gin rummy. Usually she wants to tell me what they did, but a few times I got 'yeah, it was OK' and decided not to pursue it. I don't pry, one reason being I don't want him to pry." Carole shook her head, smiling sadly. "That is, should I ever have something going on in my life interesting enough to pry into."

"So your daughter seems to have accepted the separation

of her parents with calmness, some maturity."

"That is the right phrase, Doctor, 'seems to.' Is there something going on underneath? Is there a surprise coming? Maybe a volcano? Is this going to make her more skeptical about love, about men and marriage? Will she pay a price for her parents' divorce?"

"After years of study and practice I can answer with great assurance that nobody knows."

Carole smiled, shook her head in mock despair.

"Children growing up today know that people get divorced. If not their parents, then their friends' parents, and all the movie stars and princes and millionaires that fill the headlines. Children react to family problems, family breakups, in as many ways as adults do. A lot, obviously, depends on the nature of the divorce -- the style, if you will. Physical or verbal abuse, things thrown, shouting; these mark a child, can scar deeply. Since neither you nor Ken ever mentioned such actions I assume they aren't happening."

"No, a few tears, but nothing ugly. And Jamie wasn't even home during the worst discussion."

"So what is she seeing, what is being modeled for her? The two adults she loves most dealing with a difficult, challenging personal situation in a civil manner. Not a bad thing for a child to see. Would it be better if she saw only love till death does part her parents? Sure, but that doesn't mean she will suffer great harm from the divorce."

"But there may be some harm" Carole said with a worried look.

"Of course. What you should do is what I suspect you are already doing. Check in with her as she permits, ask her how she is doing but be prepared to accept 'fine' as an answer. Trust your mothering instincts. You have a good relationship, talk to each other?"

"Yes."

"Then I repeat, trust your mothering instincts. While there are no guarantees, it is unlikely that she will abruptly stop communicating and begin acting out. What you may see, hear, are hints."

"Such as--"

"Small problems suddenly viewed as large. Getting frustrated more quickly or easily than you are used to seeing. Communication with you slipping, grades slipping. Misdirected or inappropriate anger. Insomnia, nightmares, baby talk or acting less mature than usual."

The look of worry on Carole's face deepened. "What a list!"

"The main thing, Carole, is to watch for these, to recognize them as symptoms of something underneath. Be patient, be accessible. Tell her you love her. Sometimes the words 'I love you' are the best therapy in the world, but they don't jump to mind as the thing to say when your child has suddenly started failing mathematics or refusing to turn the music down without a fight."

"I'll be alert, I promise. And patient and loving."

"From the way you relate things I really don't anticipate big problems, but should that happen I know people who specialize in teenage angst -- and are very good at it. Now before we run out of time, I do want to talk a bit more about how you are feeling about romance, about love."

"A new love?"

Dr. Ckeye nodded.

"Do you mean ready to look or ready to fall?"

"Yes."

Carole set her glass down on its pewter coaster, put both hands on the arms of the chair and sighed a long, deep, releasing sigh. She looked at the doctor, who had a slight smile on her lips.

"I'll bet you've heard sighs like that before."

"Many, many times. It is almost always a good sign, a change. What did you call it, a turning point? Let's put a name on it, a turning point sigh. Next person who does that I'll say 'ahh, a turning point sigh.' In this case it means --"

Another, smaller sigh. "Means I am ready to date, to find someone, to have him find me."

"I think so too. I wish you the greatest success. Not that I anticipate problems, but I will be here if you need me."

"Oh dear, I can't stand it, I have to ask. Aren't you ever going to retire? No, that isn't the question, its--"

"I am eighty-one, I love what I do, I help people and gain strength from that every day. I work fewer hours than I used to, but I cannot imagine retiring."

"You are a wonderful lady."

"Thank you. So are you, Carole, so are you. Stop in the middle of brushing your teeth tonight to tell yourself that. Say it when you are falling asleep or while you are working. Say 'I am a wonderful lady.' I told you about the psychic energy tanks, and you thought that made sense."

"Yes."

"Here is another. I know it sounds a bit cute, pop psychology, but I am totally convinced of its validity. If you feel that way about yourself it shows through, and other people sense it. Glow, aura, vibrations, soul, essence; if you believe you are a good person, a person of value to others, really inculcate that belief into your mental makeup, then people will perceive it -- they will see you as you see yourself."

"I'm going to be just dandy fine, like that?"

"Present tense, and more emphasis."

"I am dandy fine!"

"Yes you am. And are."

Chapter Twenty-Three

Carole moved rapidly through the familiar aisles of the supermarket. Shopping had changed since Ken moved out; more salads and pasta, less beef. Jamie voiced the occasional complaint since she had her father's taste for red meat, but seafood and chicken were more often on the table.

Turning the corner and heading down the canned fruit and vegetable aisle, applesauce and jellied cranberries frequent side dishes that had to be replenished, Carole's cart came within inches of colliding with Trudy's.

"Well hello, Carole. Haven't seen you since the Exford's New Year's party. Got something cooking, was going to call you soon."

"Then this is an opportune meeting, Trudy. I was going to give you a call. Free tonight?"

"Sure, phone or in person?"

"I'll brave the cold."

"No, let me. I have to make a run this evening, pick something up, so I'll park and come over. How about I show up around eight and you have something warm to drink?"

"Options. Tea, coffee, chocolate, hot toddy if I can remember how--"

Trudy moved her cart to let several people go by.

"Got to shed me some party pounds. Tea, no sugar. Most sad, but I'm jiggling more than I want to."

"I will tea no sugar with you. Eight-ish."

"See you."

By eight the stars were bright overhead, the cloudless sky letting what heat had accumulated during the sunny day go straight up. Although spring was coming soon, it was five degrees when Trudy parked her car and walked across the street.

"Don't you love these Massachusetts winters? So invigorating."

"If the invigoration ended by March 15, state law, I would love them more. Sometimes spring takes forever. Give me your coat, have a seat, tea in a few minutes."

Jamie came bounding down the stairs.

"Honey, do you remember Mrs. Miller?"

"Hello Jamie. I'm sure everyone comments on how you're growing, but I'll add to the chorus. You are becoming one lovely young lady."

"Thank you Mrs. Miller. Mom, do we have any ice cream?"

Trudy groaned.

"I'm sorry, you are victim to another one of my diets. But there are still some of your Aunt Ernestine's pecan cookies in the freezer. Just don't eat them where I can see."

"Mom, you can have one."

"Yes I can. And so can Mrs. Miller, to help her ward off the cold on her way home."

Trudy nodded acceptance.

"And turn on the stove, please. I already filled the kettle."

Carole and Trudy sat down as Jamie headed for the kitchen.

"Let me give you the party invitation before I forget. A bunch of the crowd are getting together for a 'shake the late winter blues' party week from Saturday at the Rockery. Some of the same folks you met when we went last time, some new faces. Some mellow, some weird, some desperate, all single. You need a pep talk on getting out and meeting new people?"

"No, and that is why I was going to call you. And who can resist mellow weird desperate singles? I've done my mourning, been to my counselor, and it is time to meet new people. Is people a euphemism for men?"

"Mostly, although it could be a woman who has a brother or cousin. Or ex she's trying to fix up so he'll leave her alone. So no pep talk, you'll be there? Most splendid. Want to ride together?"

"Is this that thing about single women riding together so if the riders get lucky they can accept a ride from a gentleman?"

"You are so new to this, I'm going to have to mother hen you to keep my conscience clear. They aren't all gentlemen, and unfortunately you can't tell the good from the bad, the mellow from the weird, while making small talk over rock and roll. So lucky is also a dubious proposition."

"Safely I'll go home with you."

"Or not. Prince Charming his own self might be there."

"Horse in the parking lot."

While they were laughing Jamie appeared with a tray. It held a cozy-covered teapot, two teacups on saucers with spoons, two cookies on a separate dish, two cloth napkins and the silver sugar bowl. She moved carefully, setting it down on the coffee table in front of Trudy.

Carole smiled warmly at Jamie. "Thank you, Honey."

"Yes, thank you."

"My pleasure. Just like it's Mom's pleasure to let me go to the Cognitive Dissonance concert."

"Still under discussion, dear."

Jamie made a disgusted face and returned to the kitchen, got three cookies and a glass of milk and went back to her room.

"I am supposed to approve my baby going to a rock concert where people mash or mosh or whatever that is. You know there are drugs there, crazies. She is not accepting 'no' and I think a storm is brewing."

"She telling you all her friends are going?"

"Well, the truth is some are. Twelve, thirteen, fourteen-year-olds. The boys, Cognitive Dissonance, are only something like sixteen or seventeen, so it's the right age group, but I am just scared to death."

"Ken weigh in, or do you make all these decisions?"

"I'm waiting for that. Mostly I make the decisions about activities; he doesn't mind, but we haven't had a brick wall like this before. I am dead against it and she's determined to go. So Ken will have to weigh in, can't duck this one. I don't think she's asked him yet, but that's coming for sure. Could be a problem. No -- will be a problem, whatever he says."

"You might try 'wait until you have children, you'll understand!' One of my mother's favorite lines."

"Didn't work at all on you, did it?"

"Zero."

They sat a moment, sipped their tea, no sugar. The cookies were rich with butter and pecans.

"You said you were going to call me. Remember, when we almost collided today?"

"Kinda said it already. I have mourned the man and marriage, visited the good doctor, got my courage cranked up a bit, and I am getting lonely. Lonelier. Horny, too. Ready for a Trudy fix-up, a Trudy special."

"Not too special, or I'll grab him myself. Now about that horny. Can Jamie hear us?"

"Can't you hear that music? That's the latest CDCD."

"Huh?"

"CDCD. I had to say 'huh' myself, which earned me a 'you are so very old' look from Jamie, explanation being Cognitive Dissonance Compact Disk. All the cool people know that -- cool meaning much younger than I am, or maybe ever was. It's usually played much louder than that, guess she is making a concession to my having a guest, but regardless of volume it's played many times too many. Like I said, storm brewing. No, her door is shut, the teenage boys do rock, and she certainly can't hear us."

"Good. You mentioned horny. Well, you ab-so-lute-ly can get laid if you're in the mood, lots of volunteers. Bad lovers, overweight and come in a minute, plenty of those. Good lovers, know how to be good to you, for you, and not tell all their friends afterward -- those are few and far between. Great lovers only in the romance novels, I fear, or maybe one out of a thousand, and I'm only on number one-hundred thirty-seven. But sex is available."

"Maybe I'm not so horny."

"Hey, what happens happens. I'm glad you're thinking about meeting men, dating."

"Not sure I'm ready for hot pursuit yet, but like you said, what happens happens. So I'm going to mix and mingle--"

"Hoping to mix and match?"

"Cute. But I'm on the scene, shaking the hand, laughing at the joke. New ideas, new faces, change the pace. Maybe connect, but certainly mingle."

"I understand you're planning on taking it slow, but lots of the men, and all the women in our social swim are looking for the big C."

"Commitment."

"So fast you learn. Yep, which means if a live one shows up you have to make your move or get out of the way because you will be trampled by the hungry hordes."

"Forget horny."

"No, don't forget it, get out there, strut your stuff. Doesn't mean you are constantly prowling, doesn't mean you can't relax and enjoy a party or group without looking up every time the door opens, the way most men do. Do I need to say again what happens happens?"

Carole was in mid-sip and started to laugh, choking slightly.

"Nope, got it."

"There are no prospects? All those people you work with, your friends and friends' second cousins, you haven't been introduced to or met anyone?"

"One nice guy, I shot him down twice. Not ready, I said. See you around, he said. I'll bet he is long since married, or at least gobbled up."

"What the hey, give him a call. Might be on the rebound, broken heart waiting for your healing words. Healing hands. Healing--"

"I get it, I get it" Carole said, both laughing.

"Actually, my counselor said the same thing. Give him a call."

"So?"

"I think I'm ready to move on, but your party sounds like a good test. Our secret, it will be my coming-out party."

"You're a little bit mature to be a debutante. And aren't they all virgins, or supposed to be? But if this is your reentry into dating, fine. Our secret, Carole's coming out party. And it isn't my party. A bunch of folks getting together, dance, drink, be warm in the cold."

"Can't you picture cave dwellers doing that? After they killed a woolly mammoth or some other great beast they got together to dance, drink, be warm in the cold."

"No deodorant, no birth control, no perms. Dance and drink and do it in the back of the cave.'"

"Great name for a motel, one of those by-the-hour places. Back Of The Cave."

The teenage boys and their bubbling professions of yearning and love were suddenly louder as Jamie emerged from her room with empty glass and plate. She ran by them, went into the kitchen and emerged with an apple, then returned to her room with a too-firm closing of her door.

"This too shall pass, Mom."

"Eventually. But the concert doth loom."

Trudy soon headed home through the cold, crisp night. Carole cleaned up a bit then made sure the doors were locked, the lights off, the thermostat set for the evening. She went up the stairs and knocked on Jamie's door.

"Come in."

Carole opened the door. "Thanks again for serving us."

Jamie grunted. She was on her bed reading, curled up with her back to the door. She didn't look up from her book.

"Goodnight?"

"Everything is just fine for you, isn't it?"

Carole was surprised by the upset in Jamie's voice. "What everything, what do you mean?"

"You've got friends, Dad has friends. You both act like this is the way it is and who cares."

Jamie's room has two chairs. One is a used office chair bought by Carole from her company, used for homework at the desk. The other is a wooden rocker, with cloth seat and back, purchased by Ken for Carole when she became pregnant, appropriated by Jamie several years ago. Carole sat in the rocker.

"If we're going to have a fight can you at least look at me?"

"What if I don't want to?"

"Then I can either leave or talk to your back."

Jamie didn't respond. Carole sat, rocking gently.

"Jamie, is there something that your father isn't doing, or me, I don't understand you when you say 'who cares?'" I care, your father cares. Is this about the concert or something else?"

"I wannabe a regular kid like I was. You and Daddy had to go and get divorced and now everything is all a mess."

"Please turn the music down, it's hard to talk."

Jamie reached behind her without looking, found the volume control and turned it down. A little.

"Thank you. Now, what is all a mess? I don't know what you want. What are you mad about? And would you please turn around?"

Jamie turned over on her other side in an even tighter fetal position.

"It's this whole thing with you and Dad. I mean my time. I feel like I have to be with you, 'cause you're sharing me and if I don't spend time with you then you don't get your share. And I like being with Daddy but sometimes he wants to group date with somebody he's dating and it's OK sometimes but not always. And he wants his share, I know he loves me, so how do I say 'not tonight, I want to hang with my friends' without hurting his feelings or causing a big problem with you and him. A time fight problem. And you used to have Dad at home. I mean, Daddy goes out on dates sometimes and you don't. And I feel guilty if I leave you here alone."

Carole worked hard to keep her emotions off her face. "Honey, we're divorced. I'm going to be alone sometimes, that's just the way it is. But I'm also going to be out with Trudy Miller and other friends, folks from work. And I plan on dating, maybe meeting someone, I don't know, but dating. As for your father and time with him, I can talk to him about it or you can. I understand you want to do your own thing, and I'm sure he understands that too, but we both want our precious Jamie minutes. I guess that puts pressure on you, and I'm sorry."

"But it isn't just that. That's what I meant about being such a mess. It's a problem for me if I don't give you guys your time, but then if you want to go out on a date or something you have to worry about me, you know, can you go out when it's your turn to be the keeper. I feel like an egg or something you guys keep handing back and forth."

Carole looked at Jamie tenderly. "Sweet thing, that's exactly what you are. There is no way to describe what, how we feel about you, your father and I. I know you don't want to hear it, but until you have children of your own you can't understand. I don't object to the concert because of the goopy music--"

"Young music."

"Wonderful young music, pure cotton candy. I'm sorry, I'll quit. My objection is concern about your safety. Having to juggle our schedules is what we want to do. We want to be with you."

Jamie sat up, moved to the edge of the bed, her legs hanging down. "But it's like I have a responsibility to be with you, with you and Dad I mean, to give you your share of me. Before you guys split there wasn't any of this, now it's all 'who's turn is it?' So when's it my turn?"

Carole sighed, shook her head slightly. "You remember Tom from my job, he and his wife Gracie came to dinner once? He has a thing he likes to say, A-ly and B-ly. So, A-ly, I want you to tell me what is bothering you. Always always. If I get a little upset or worried that's fine, I'd much rather worry about what I know than try to guess what's wrong. 'Keep open the doors of communication' it says on page thirty-seven of the instruction book that comes with new babies."

"No such book!"

"No such, learn on the fly. But let me continue with item B. B-ly, we love you so very much. You are going to be gone fairly soon, the only child, so I won't have a child at home anymore. So part of it is being selfish about that. I'm sure your father feels the same. And part is what we said, we have to worry about you, watch over you, that's our job. Instincts as much as anything. Protect the young."

"But not too much, OK?"

"I have to protect you all the time, every minute, smother you. Have to! But I'll try to ease up a little."

"Daddy too?"

"Jamie, he wants to see you too. I'm not crazy about speaking for him. He's the one who wanted to leave, but I guess I'd ask you to try to understand. You live here, which means I get to see you lots more than he does, even if you're only on your way to the refrigerator. By the way, you need new shoes again, don't you?"

"I promise to stop growing by the time you have to pay for college."

"I'm holding you to that promise. It may be one or the other, new clothes and shoes or tuition, not both. Where were we?"

"Easing up on the egg. Less scrambling."

"That's terrible!" Carole laughed. "Look, I can't make any promises. No, I can say it better. I can't be sure I'll pick up on everything, know when you want to be with your friends, your dad can't either. You'll have to tell us. We'll have to listen. We do want our Jamie minutes, will want them when you are married and running the country--"

"Drop out, marry rich man, eat ice cream all day."

"Over dead body. Bodies, mine and your father's. But let's all three of us work at not making too big a deal of this. Keep aware, easy on the egg."

"Sunny side up."

"I love being your straight man."

"Woman."

"You've had too many cookies, your sugar is showing. Speaking of which, thanks again for the tea service. I love showing off my well-mannered child."

"Ain't no thing."

"Ain't no thing? Does that mean the same as 'my pleasure?'"

"You're getting it, Mom. I'm proud of you."

"Enough." Carole got up, walked to the bed, gave Jamie a tight hug and two kisses and left, ignoring the electronic drumbeat that filled the room. As she closed the door she heard the music turned down a little more.

Chapter Twenty-Four

Mid-April. Spring for most of the country, but in northeast America winter lingered. A great low pressure system, hundreds of miles across, turned slowly, almost gracefully counterclockwise, took warmer air from North Virginia, Maryland and the surrounding area, carried it out to sea to pick up a load of moisture, then back again over greater Boston. Fat wet flakes fell and fell, not enough to stop the commuters or close the schools but enough to make everyone late. The benefit was a sense of hush, the world made bright and white and quiet by billions of little pillows and lace doilies.

Carole sat in her office and looked out at the snow dropping gently past her window. Resolved, she turned, picked up the phone, pushed the buttons.

"Tocar Products, Ralph Donnell speaking. May I help you?"

"Ralph, its Carole Tagee. How are you?"

A brief pause. She was about to ask if he remembered her when he said "Well, surprised, I guess. How are you?"

"I'm fine." In a bit of a rush "I'd like to see you again. If you'd like. Unless you're tied up -- seeing someone else, I mean."

"Well, I am seeing someone, but not -- yes, I'd like to see you again. What did you have in mind?"

"You said you liked courtroom intrigue books. Have you

seen the new movie with that name?"

"Courtroom Intrigue. No, but I was planning on it."

"It should be here at least two more weeks. My treat. Popcorn, even. What's your pleasure?"

An answer to the question flashed through his brain, the kind Tom would have appreciated. Out loud he said "Not this weekend but next. Friday or Sunday, your choice."

"Friday. I'll even drive."

"Well, if you insist. Old fashioned me. I can get to the tickets and popcorn, but gosh gee willikers, shouldn't the guy drive? I'd really rather if you don't mind."

"Gosh gee willikers? All right, I don't want to upset old-fashioned you. My address is two three two one two Fulton Parkway. I live about twenty minutes from Cinema Six, Friday movies start at seven-thirty. Time to meet my daughter if she's home, allow for snow, how is six-thirty?"

"Six-thirty is fine. Six-thirty, week from Friday, boy drives girl pays. Cinematic legal maneuvers at seven thirty." A brief pause, then he added "I'm glad you called. Maybe someday you'll tell me why my stock has gone up after six months. Someday."

Silence. Ralph waited.

Softer. "Maybe after the movie we can go for a drink. Or a chocolate soda. We can talk about your stock rating then, if you like."

"I like talking to you, Carole." He heard in his head, but did not say, "I remember liking you."

What he said was "I'm glad you called. See you then."

"See you then. Goodbye."

The snow kept falling, though a little lighter. The storm was easing. Carole looked at the twirling flakes, smiled.

By date night Friday the storm had been over for more than a week, the streets were clear and dry. Ralph was dressed in black slacks, dark blue shirt, and a cardigan sweater of black, blue and gray. The fates, howling with laughter and slapping their thighs, dressed Carole in black skirt, gray blouse, and a V-necked sweater of black, blue and gray.

Ralph pulled into the driveway right on time. He was wearing a pea coat and navy wool cap. He walked to the front door, rang the doorbell, and Carole opened the door. He stepped into the small hallway, removing his cap.

"I'm ready to go, but I would like you to meet my Jamie."

Carole walked to the stairs and called up to her daughter. Ralph unbuttoned his coat, but didn't catch the fashion situation. As Carole turned towards Ralph, Jamie came down the stairs, both females spotting the similarities at once. Carole stopped and her eyes widened a bit as Jamie said "Hi" and smiled, a 'caught you' smile. Ralph was sure his fly was open. He was about to turn away and check, tempted to just walk out the door and fall face down in the spring mud and lingering snow, when Carole said "I could change quickly, if you like."

Light bulb for Ralph. Not unzipped. Wash of relief. "You look fine. I'll tell anyone we meet that you're my sister. You must be Jamie. Hello. I'm Ralph Donnell."

"Hello. I like your clothes."

"I like your wit. Your mother's daughter, she scores on me too."

Beat.

"Time to go. Honey, we'll be--"

"At the Cinema Six, seeing Courtroom Intrigue, a snack afterwards if you aren't bored."

"James!" To Ralph "I did not say that."

Ralph helped Carole with her coat, no hat, good-byes and nice-to-meet-you were said. As Ralph followed Carole down the walk he checked his fly, just in case. Zipped.

The movie was good, lots of twists and turns, handsome rich bad guys in expensive suits losing in the end. The dating two shared a tub of popcorn, passing it back and forth, their hands occasionally touching. Walking out they both said they were thirsty. Where to go?

"Well, I've had an image of a chocolate soda since you mentioned it. We can certainly go for a drink, a bar-type drink, but a sody in a booth would be a pleasure."

"Sody?"

"Vanilla ice cream, chocolate syrup, soda water. Are we there?"

"We can certainly be there, but do I have to call it a sody?"

"No, although the booth is mandatory."

They found an ice cream store. Carole got the soda, but Ralph saw a luscious picture of a tin roof sundae and ordered one.

"Fugue for tin roof" Carole said.

"What?"

"Bad joke. In the pool last year, you told me about Fugue for Tinhorns. Tinhorn, tin roof. Sorry."

"No, that's good. What a memory. That conversation was a long time ago."

Time out for ice cream.

"Want to talk about the stock market?"

"Any stock in particular?"

"Mine, remember? Why did my stock go up? Why did you call me, Carole?"

She stuck the spoon in her glass, took out a generous scoop of ice cream, ate it. "My husband didn't leave me for another. He was -- there was a woman, but he made it really clear that she was just a diversion. You should know, Ralph, that I was set aside. Discarded. I don't know much about your marriage, a little from Tom, but it was short, right?"

"Very short, no fault, just a mutual mistake."

"Still, it must have hurt some. I'm not making light of it."

"I know."

"The answer to your stock valuation question has nothing to do with you. Wait, that didn't sound the way I wanted it to. Better answer. I liked you from the moment we met, liked the way we talked to each other. I remember that lunch, assume you do."

"Of course. Light conversation, heavy garlic."

"Did I seem distracted, a little fuzzy?"

"No, although I confess I saw you walking towards the restaurant and you looked like the weight was pretty heavy."

"Guess I'm a decent actress. All through that lunch my husband, things he'd said, things we had done, kept popping into my head. So when I said I wasn't ready I was just that, too full of self-pity, too upset, too much Ken in my head to date you. Loving him and wanting to kill him at the same time, I guess. That devastating feeling that you are a left-over."

"So this date means that, uh, your head is behaving."

"Not nuts anymore, you mean. I needed time, Ralph. I needed time and counseling. Took some time, got some counseling. Went to a women's discussion group. Lots of problems with you men!"

"Sorry."

"Not all your fault. I think. So you see, Ralph Donnell, it isn't that your stock went up. It is that I was ready to get in the market."

"Lots of stocks, lots of markets. NYSE, NASDAQ, Chicago --"

"Change of metaphor. Toe in the water. You are my first."

"Toe?"

"So much for that metaphor. I give."

"How about when you felt you were ready to date you decided to call me first?"

"When I felt I was ready to date I decided to call you first."

Chapter Twenty-Five

The regulars were all there looking for a new face, a new chance. There were some newer faces, Carole's being one. But mostly it was the same people reconsidering the same people; those they flirted or dated or slept with last week, month, year. All but a few had been married once. The never-married were looked at with suspicion, the multiple-married as high risk. It was safe at the usual place with the usual prospects, but those really looking would have to break away, find a new place to seek a mate.

The combination of early and aggressive phone calls by Trudy and a few of her friends, late winter cabin fever and a clear night had produced a great turnout, fifteen women and ten men. After about a half hour several of the men began looking at their watches, considering where better they might go on this Saturday night. Where could they find whatever they're looking for. The party plan was for everyone to assemble by eight. All fifteen actually were together for a few minutes -- those late to arrive getting to the Rockery by eight-thirty, the early leavers still consulting their watches and itches. Carole danced with three men, laughed at jokes, had two vodka-and-lemonades.

By nine several of the men had left. By nine fifteen the women began leaving in groups of two and three. The Rockery was rocking, the dancing man holding forth in his silent manner, the beer flowing. But something new, action, a one-nighter, or heaven willing he/she of the big C were to be found somewhere else, gotta keep looking. Trudy and Carole left at nine-thirty, went to another singles bar, a place known for assignations and rendezvous by those over thirty.

"Great place" said Trudy. "The parking lot is littered with wedding rings."

"Perfect. I so want to find me a cheating man."

Trudy was driving, so she ordered coffee. Carole had one too, decaf. The waitress was quick to take and deliver the orders; two women drinking coffee did not indicate big tips.

"So what do you think? Spot any likelies?"

"I don't know how to do this. I can't get used to -- start over. I can't figure out how to have a pleasant conversation with a man while music plays and people shout and laugh and there is too much cigarette smoke and I'm getting a bit tipsy. Drink and I'm not so sure of myself. Not drink and I seem like a prude."

"This is just about meeting. A man and a woman in a bar, they meet, exchange phone numbers, follow up. I don't think about making a winning sales pitch at the Rockery or places like this; hello and phone number are the essentials, a little chat maybe, but it takes a date to check him out. For him to check me out."

They sat a while, sipped coffee which the waitress had refilled, her hopes of a good tip not all lost. People danced, laughed, flirted, drank, looked up each time the door opened.

"I hate my life" Trudy said softly, her eyes toward the dance floor. "I am so fucking tired of this. I never want to be in another bar as long as I live." She turned towards Carole, her eyes moist, her face hard. "I'm sorry, here I am supposed to mother-hen you and instead we do therapy."

"Trudy--"

"I think I am going to try the personals again. And sign up for one of those lunch date fix-up services. He isn't here, Carole. Not in a bar."

"The friend you told me about, getting married--"

"Just got, last week. Honeymoon at Niagara Falls! Like a coupla kids, can you believe it? Couldn't stay long at the reception, if I heard her giggle one more time I was going to have to slap her."

"Where'd she find him? That sounds like a shopping trip. Where did they meet?"

"Where'd she find him works fine, it is shopping. They met at a bar. He's there with two friends, she is too. One of her friends knows one of his group, use to live next door or something. So the two old neighbors hug, everyone gathers around, three women, three men, they get one big table, phone numbers fly, before you know it she's got the ring, in bed in Niagara Falls, giggling no doubt."

"So this does work sometimes. Not talking you into it, because I'm certainly not crazy about bars, but she found--"

"Found him in a bar. Yes she did. Makes one crazy, it does. Like slot machines, you think that this is a big waste of time and money, and then the lady next to you hits and the silver dollars fly and you think it is your turn next, could be. Got to be. Got to be!"

"You've tried personals before? You didn't tell me that."

"Answered a few. One nice guy, two dates and I was getting pretty interested. Sex third date as far as I was concerned. Never happened. Went back to his wife. Told me he was divorced, but really just separated."

"Jerk."

"Not a total jerk. Total jerks are the ones where it seems like something is happening and then they disappear, not a trace. No, this guy actually called and sorta apologized, said he liked me swell. Swell. I remember him using that word. Liked me swell, sorry about lying, his wife begged him to come back, she'd change, they could work it out, like that. I never had a chance. Wish I could have gotten him into bed, might have given his old lady a run for her money."

"You place any ads?"

"Once in the City Monthly. Three or four letters, some phone calls, one date. Nothing. But I've been reading the ads about those lunch meeting services and those places where you videotape your sales pitch, and I'm about ready to invest in one or the other. Maybe both, I don't know, not very expensive. But I've gotta cut down on making the bar scene. Too fucking depressing and cold, and I for sure don't want to get too fond of drinking. Besides, those peanut snacks and drinks put the jiggle on. Men don't have to worry about those jiggling pounds the way women do. How did that rule get written?"

"Do you really want to start on that one tonight?"

"No. Not ever, too depressing. Sorry, Carole, sorry to have the evening end like this."

"You going to be all right?"

Trudy was wiping her eyes, not really crying but close. She stopped abruptly and stared at Carole.

"Was that a polite way of asking if I might kill myself?"

"No, well maybe a little, you did say you hated your life."

"Bless you. You are a good friend. No, not to worry, I'm blue about the wedding, I guess, and about tonight. Got all cranked up about getting a bunch of us together and then the reality was, it was mostly the regulars and everybody split for another bar, another shopping trip. I'm surprised none of them are here, haven't seen any."

"Me either."

"But no killing of self. Not anywhere near that depressed."

"Ready to leave? Want to stay, talk some more?"

"No, that's enough."

"But I do want to say that this did what I wanted, gave me a going-out experience --- wait, vodka and coffee don't mix. I meant a coming out experience, really doing it, being a divorced lady checking out those divorced men. Getting me started the way I told my counselor I would."

"Good counselor?"

"Amazing. Dr. Ckeye, she's this classy, old-fashioned

lady, eighty-one. I hope I look half that good if I make it to eighty-one. She must have been some beauty in grad school. I like her a lot. She's semi-retired but might take you on."

"You think I need counseling."

"It scares me to hear someone say they hate their life. I know she helped me. Too pushy?"

"Not too pushy. Friend. Let's get out of here."

The next Tuesday the phone rang.

"Hello, Carole? Hi. This is Philip Peterson. Phil. Met at the Rockery last week, friend of Trudy's, we danced to Summertime Blues, remember?"

"Sure, how are you?"

"Fine, fine. And you?"

"Also fine, thanks."

A pause.

"I wondered if you'd like to go out this weekend."

"Well, ah, what did you have in mind?"

"Movie, maybe?"

"Sure, I like movies."

A slightly longer pause.

"I'm not sure what's playing but I could check and call you back."

"OK, um, I have a daughter, need to make plans for her. What night did you have in mind?"

"Friday or Saturday. Or Sunday."

"I'd prefer Saturday or Sunday."

"Not Friday. That's OK, that's OK. I'll call you back, let me check the paper, see what's playing and I'll call back."

"Thank you, Phil. That'll be fine."

They said goodbye and hung up. "My goodness, I have an almost date" she said aloud. Carole considered calling Trudy to ask about Phil but thought better of it; might not help Trudy's mood to know she had gotten a call.

They settled on Saturday night. Carole had a vague recollection of a rule about not being available the upcoming

Saturday, ever, because that marked you as a girl sitting home alone, and if you're home alone then nobody wants you, so why should he? Carole shrugged it off, might be a good game for a girl to play but she was a grown woman and not interested in deceit. After all, he had been available the upcoming Saturday and not ashamed of it, why should she be? Another double standard like the jiggling pounds?

They chose a movie neither had seen, a polite romance set in the late eighteen hundreds, enjoyed the movie, went for a drink afterward. Carole found conversation a bit difficult with Phil, not a lot in common, but he was pleasant enough to be with.

The next Wednesday Trudy called. "Did you see my ad? No, you probably aren't reading the 'Men Wanted' personals."

"You ran an ad? Where, when?"

"Sunday's paper, week ago. I'll read it to you. Got a minute?"

"Sure. You sure sound happier than last time we spoke."

"Weepy in a bar? Try not to do that again. Shook it off, purged the blues, staring over! I ran the ad and I'm signing up for one of the connection services. Not sure which one, but I called every ad I saw and asked for a brochure. Got them spread out like travel folders, make a choice or two, get my hair done, and have at it."

"Love hearing it. Might join you, who knows. But tell me about your ad!"

"Energetic lady, five-five, still not forty, no children, seeks man for friendship and more. I love to cook. Letters only. Box 459."

"'I love to cook'?"

"Sure, why not? It's true, and I noticed none of my competition said that, so bring on those hungry men. I figured 'energetic' was code for 'good in bed.'"

"Any responses yet, or too early?"

"They mail out the responses end of the day Tuesdays and Fridays. I got three letters, Carole, came in Monday and today, so those boys must have responded the day they read my ad or the next. Hot stuff. Must have been the cooking."

"Or the energetic. Going to respond?"

"Two of them. One went to great lengths to tell me about his sensitive stomach and his special dietary needs."

Carole laughed. "The cooking caught his eye, that's for sure."

"He needs a dietician or a nurse. Maybe both. Not me."

"The other two?"

"A mason, bricklayer, owns his own company, three employees, widowed, two teenagers. Sounded like a regular guy, likes to camp out, which I can take only a little of, likes Las Vegas, which I can take a lot of, especially in the winter. Definite maybe, going to call that Bricklayer. Don't say it."

"Too obvious. The other?"

"Divorced teacher, mathematics. Not my best subject. Three kids, live with mom. Weekend visits, the usual drill. I'll tell you, Carole, I have heard as many horror stories about steps-moms as I have good stories. I'm going to call him too, but he will have to dazzle me with more than mathematics. If it seems like a possibility I'll meet the kids, step cautiously. Maybe get advice from your doctor, Sky, is it?"

"Pronounced that way, spelled C- K- E- Y- E."

"Yeah, maybe I'll go see her if anything develops. If the math man and I can figure it out."

"Or lay the brick. You started it."

Two weeks after Carole's date with Phil he called again, and she agreed to another date. They went to a community playhouse and saw a new work about inter-generational tensions and reconciliations. As on their first date they went out afterward, and Carole found conversation was some easier this time. She also found she thought of Ralph, made comparisons. It was easier being with Ralph, conversation more natural. She missed Ralph.

That same night Ralph was with Carmen. She had called him two weeks earlier, begged him to be her date at a business-oriented reception she had to attend to maintain some important connections. They went to the rather boring event, ate lots of shrimp and crabmeat and drank generic white and red wines. Carmen shook the requisite hands and got her attendance card stamped. More habit than anything else, they went to her apartment, to bed. In her he started to say "Carole" but changed it at the last moment. Fortunately both names start with the same sound. He didn't stay the night; driving home he thought of Carole.

The following morning Ralph called Carole, told her he had been thinking about her, although not where he was while doing the thinking. He asked her to dinner and she accepted. They went to a movie with Jamie, which she referred to as a "group date." Another dinner, another group date, Ralph calling her, Carole calling him. She declined Phil, Ralph dumped Carmen.

On the two group dates the interaction between Ralph and Jamie was pleasant though neutral. He didn't work at winning her; since he never had a daughter or younger sister or even female cousin he had no idea what the right or wrong words were. He found he could ask her about school and they would have a pleasant though brief discussion. Her movie reviews, however, were detailed, and he enjoyed them and told her so. A few times they got into intense conversations about an actor or actress or the story line. After the second movie they sat in an ice cream shop and talked about the complicated plot. Jamie said "Didju see when the guy felloff the boat and allhisstuff, glasses and everything, went flying? Then the next thing we see is him walking around wearing his glasses like nothin' happened atall. Did they float or something?"

"Maybe he had an extra pair at the hotel" Ralph offered.

"Yeah, right" was her crushing retort.

Ralph called. "Carole, I've been thinking about your debate with Jamie, her attending the Cognitive Dissonance concert."

"The tickets are all sold, long since gone, but one of her friends bought a ticket for Jamie, bought it with her babysitting earnings. Little entrepreneur, if Jamie doesn't buy it from her she can scalp it for at least double what she paid."

"Smart kid."

"I am caught in a classic 'other kids can' conflict. Jamie is getting maximum mileage out of this one. Her latest is that the other parents love their children as much but trust them more. I tell her it isn't about trusting her but worries about the thousands of others who will be there. The tough thing, Ralph, is that we almost never have prolonged disagreements, but this one has gone on for over a month and it's making me crazy."

"I checked, and there will be only seating, no open area, no dancing or mosh pit. They are going to limit the sales to the number of seats, so the entrepreneur is on the right track. They are going to have heavy security, too. I called the theater manager, pretended to be a worried parent."

"So you think I should let her go."

"Nothing like advice from a childless adult to a parent, but yes, that's my vote. You know the other girls?"

"They're fine. Well, if there is no open dancing area, and good security, then I guess she may escape with her life."

"How are they getting there?"

"One mother dropping them off, another picking her up."

"Yeah, let her go."

Later that day Jamie came crashing into the house, grabbed two cookies, a bunch of grapes, and headed for her room.

"Jamie, wait a minute, I've got something to tell you, think you're going to like this."

Jamie stopped in mid-stride, turned back towards her mother. She had a half cookie in her mouth and was unable to respond except by raising her eyebrows.

"I've been thinking it over. Actually, I talked it over with Ralph. He thinks, we think you should go see CD. I said it right, didn't I?"

Jamie swallowed quickly, ran toward her mother and wrapped her up in a big hug, grapes and cookies suffering. "Thank you thank you."

"Well, you owe some thanks to Ralph, he checked it out, it's not quite the snake pit I feared."

"Hey Ralph, points for you. I promise not to run away with the CDs like a groupie--"

"That's a relief. Now the only problem is coordinating things with your father."

"What things? I'm going to ride with Amy, her mom's got it all worked out."

"I know, that's one of the reasons I agreed, you'll be chauffeured safely. No, I mean that's his weekend."

"Wellmaybe I don't want you to work it out. Maybe I'll tell him. The egg may speak for itself."

"All right, little egg. Or maybe hatchling, testing her wings. I don't care who tells him, you or me."

"Or Ralph."

"Who is teaching you to be so very witty?"

"Why you, of course."

"Ralph isn't a choice. You or me."

"Me."

"My grownup daughter."

"My worrying mother."

Chapter Twenty-Six

"Hello, Jamie, it's Ralph. How're you doing?"

"Fine. Want to talk to my mother?"

"Yes, please."

"I'll get her."

He waited. Soon he heard a door open, and a called "Mom! Phone!" He heard a faint response, then another brief wait.

"Hello?"

"Hi, Carole. Bad time? I can call back."

"Doing yard work. Glad to stop. April showers bring May weeds."

"Less poetic but more truthful."

"Exactly. What's up?"

"I want to talk to you. Can I see you tonight?"

"Sure, come over and sit on the patio, but don't forget to tell me how nice the yard looks."

They sat on the patio. It was cool, the sun setting, but they both wore jackets and held large mugs of hot coffee. After a few minutes of light talk Carole said "Well, you scheduled this meeting. What's the agenda?"

"Have you ever been to the old city in Quebec?"

"No, I don't even know about it."

"It's wonderful. May I take you there?"

A pause. "Take me to Quebec?" Another pause. "Do you

want some more coffee?" she said, starting to rise.

"Does that mean 'no' or 'I need some time to decide'?"

Carole settled back in her chair.

"I need some time."

"Or of course it could mean 'I don't want to go any further with this relationship' or the biggie, 'I don't find you physically attractive.'"

"No, neither one Ralph. It doesn't. It's me. It's about scrambled me."

"Call me again when you're unscrambled" rehearsed in his head, but he said nothing, just looked at her. Carole got up, went to the kitchen and was gone several moments. She returned with the coffee pot and two kinds of cookies, sugar and oatmeal raisin. Ralph took one of each while Carole refilled his cup. By the time she refilled her cup and returned the pot to the kitchen he had sampled each.

"Delicious."

"Thank you. Home made."

"My compliments. Which reminds me. The yard looks great."

"Thank you again."

They continued to sit in the cool, mild air, the deepening twilight. Twin floodlights lit the patio, but only a few bugs responded to the call. Carole and Ralph were comfortable physically, uncomfortable mentally. Ralph wanted her to say yes, to explore Quebec with him, to be naked with him in a lovely room in a bed and breakfast. If she said no then he was gone, outathere, and she could call again some time. If he were still available. Carole heard voices, Trudy's the loudest, asking her exactly what was her problem. "Here is this nice guy and he wants to be with you and you are doing the mental case thing? Shape up, woman!"

Moments passed. Ralph Donnell said nothing. Carole Tagee said nothing. Cookies and coffee disappeared. Distant sounds -- parents calling, a car starting, barking dogs. Immediate sounds of coffee cups on saucers. Hearts beating.

Thoughts, decisions, choices spinning and tumbling.

"Carole, I'll tell you what I think this is. It's about us. Exploring us. Finding out if there is, should be, us. You're pushing me away again." Gently he said it, no heat or accusation.

She looked at him, looked away.

"I'm sorry, Carole. Thanks for the coffee and home cooking." Again the words said gently. He stood.

"I'd love to go" she said to her cookie plate. She raised her face towards him, smiled. "I'd love to go."

Chapter Twenty-Seven

Quebec, actually the old Quebec City within the fortress walls, is a wonderful place for lovers to explore and learn about, and to learn about each other. Once a small city of military might, it was now a place of magic and beauty. And great restaurants.

Carole called Ralph two days after she had accepted his invitation. When he heard her hello he thought she was going to back out, but she quickly assured him that she not only was going to join him, but really meant it when she said she wanted to. "One condition, Ralph. I pay for me -- travel, food and board. It has got to be that way, just has to. Please quickly say yes and then let's talk about when."

"It was my invitation---"

"Please Ralph, please. I want to go, be with you. I really want to know if--where this is going. Besides to bed." Although obvious, it was the first time either of them had acknowledged, said out loud, that they were going to share a bed. Which meant sex. Sex. Zing went the strings! Ralph was pleased, thrilled, and suddenly outrageously horny. He wanted this woman. "But I am paying for me and now let's talk about when we are going and what kind of shoes I should pack."

"All right, I agree, although you will have to let me buy you a pamplemousse."

"Depends. What is it?"

"Grapefruit in French. What a fun word to say. Pamplemousse. Pamplemousse."

Carole laughed. "Sure, please buy me two pamplemousses. Pamplemoussei. I love them."

"Well, since you want to change the subject, you mentioned something about a bed. Going to bed. Something."

"I can't get pregnant, so you, we, don't have to worry about that. No raincoats." Ralph almost asked her what she meant but then got it.

"Can we go tonight? This afternoon? In five minutes?"

Carole laughed again, easily. They started talking about dates and quickly settled on either three weeks later or five weeks later, both weekends when Jamie would be with her father. The deciding factors would be the availabilities of plane seats and accommodations. Since Ralph had already been checking on these he offered to continue his efforts, and said he would call back soon. He also asked if he could see her the next night, maybe take her and Jamie to a movie. Carole promised to call him at home that night after she had talked to her James.

After they said goodbye Carole began thinking about the warmth and desire in his voice. Long time since she heard those tones in Ken's voice, such a long time. She was pleased and flattered, feeling a heat begin that had been dormant for just as long.

The fates had been having too much fun with this relationship to miss one more opportunity for mischief. Of course nothing was available until the second open weekend, five weeks away. Five horny weeks. Without talking about it they both understood that Quebec would be where they first made love. So they went to some movies, occasionally with Jamie, some meals, some talking walks. With three weeks still to go Ralph made dinner for Carole at his apartment. As they sat sipping wine afterward he said "We're waiting until Quebec, right?"

"Yes, although a little more wine and I might change my mind. But I thought that was our romantic plan. Too corny?"

"Not at all, I love the romance. He sure doesn't."

It would have been a naughty but witty thing to say if he could have been urbane and cool, but the moment he said it he blushed, blushed as he hadn't since childhood. Seeing his blushing she pointed at his red face and laughed, which prompted him to turn even brighter red and roar with laughter.

They drank some more, talked some more. He spoke of his brief marriage and divorce. She talked about the birth of Jamie. When she left they kissed long and hard, mouths open, tasting of wine. She could feel his penis pressing against her through their clothes. Her heat jumped and flamed. They thought about each other for hours and the first thing upon waking, each in their lonely beds.

Of course the group dates ended with the two cool ladies going home together. When Carole went out with Ralph alone she always came home for the night. But now she was going to be out of town overnight, really over three nights, with Ralph. This called for a serious sit-down discussion.

Children don't want to know about their parent's sexuality, are never comfortable thinking of dad or mom in heat, in bed, doing things. They don't want to dwell on it as teenagers nor when they are in their twenties or thirties or ever. Carole knew this and didn't want to make Jamie confront, or even consider, anything that her daughter would rather not. But "We're going away together for the weekend" is a truth and also a euphemism, and Jamie would know it meant one bed for two people.

Jamie knew the basics of sex, had read some prim and modestly worded pamphlets, had asked a few questions of her mother. Carole believed in the parenting theory that when a child asks a question about sex the parent should answer directly and honestly, giving the information needed but not embellishing, using age-appropriate language. This theory was not always easy to translate into practice, but Carole did not want to lie to her child, or have to backtrack and admit to shading the truth. The sex discussions were about anatomy -- how babies are made. The personal and moral discussions were about respect for oneself and one's body, respect for others, moral codes. One of those codes was no sex without marriage. Now Carole was going to go have sex without marriage. Carole spent long hours thinking about this, wanting to say exactly the right thing.

Carole decided to take Jamie to a restaurant. A grown-up restaurant for a grown-up talk. But not too grown up. Yikes this was tricky. As she thought about it Carole found it easy to think of such wonderfully wrong things to say. "You'll understand when you're older." "Dating is different for adults." "This doesn't change a thing." Double yikes.

They went to a Mediterranean restaurant located in a warehouse district, one of many such areas in and around Boston with big box warehouse and distribution centers served by endlessly moving trucks and trains. Jamie had always been an adventuresome child when it came to food, and on this occasion she tried calamari for the first time, sharing an appetizer with her mother and eating more than half. On the table was good fresh bread, garlic-laced butter and a small dish with crisp radishes and carrots and dark olives. When the main dishes arrived, lemon-crusted sea bass for Jamie and a spicy stew of fish and vegetables for Carole, she decided it was time.

"Honey, I have to tell you something. You know I've been dating Ralph for a while, and we are starting to like each other a lot. We are planning on going away for a weekend, actually in three weeks when you're with your father."

"Yagonna marry him?"

Susan smiled. "Right to a key question. I forget, are you going to be a great scientist or a great lawyer?"

Jamie sighed a great, weary sigh and attacked the sea bass.

"Well, my freckled attorney-scientist, that is a good question, big important good question. But I don't have a good answer. Wait, that sounds wrong. I don't have any answer, because I just don't know. Except maybe. How is maybe?"

Jamie had just bitten off a large piece of the crusty bread and so could answer only with a frown and shake of her head.

"Sorry, James. Best I can do. We are dating to see if we -- if we care about -- Jamie, I'm learning too, you know. I guess first we go on some dates, which we have done, start to like each other, also done, maybe like each other a lot, maybe love each other, maybe love each other enough to get married."

"Lots of maybes, Mom."

"Most annoying when you sound so adult. Yep, lots of maybes. So this is part of that learning, that finding out."

Jamie nodded agreement, deep into her work. They ate in silence for a while. The waiter checked on them, refilled their water glasses.

As casually and lightly as she could, Carole said "I was a little worried you would be bothered by this. By our going away together. Glad you're not."

No response from Jamie. Carole was feeling a little disappointed, deciding whether to let it go when Jamie said "Mom, do you forget how old I am?"

"No I do not forget. I know exactly how old you are, fourteen. By strange coincidence I was there when you were born."

"So you know that soon I'm gonnabe going to high school, I'll be busy, then yaknow college in five years. I gotta start getting all those scientist and lawyer and doctor degrees, diplomas, all those things you and Daddy keep wanting me to get."

"They will not give you your diploma until you learn 'you know' 'going to' and 'have to'."

"Mother! Thank you! The deal is that then I will be going to someplace else, maybe far away. Daddy has girlfriends, you should have boyfriends. Or maybe a husband. Of course I wantchu --- want you to find a boyfriend or husband. If you want to marry Ralph that's cool, he's OK. I hope you have a great vacation. Where you going?"

"Quebec. The old fortress city of Quebec."

"Bet they have great sweaters there. You could bring your precious only child one if you wanted to."

"Precocious only child. Thank you for understanding, Honey. I have to get used to how grown up you are."

"As Grandma Susan says, fiddlesticks!"

Carole called and said it all in one continuous stream, unplanned, the words just spilling out. "Ken, when you have Jamie in two weeks could you please keep her Sunday night and take her to school? I'm going out of town with one of my boyfriends."

"That's fine, be sure to say hello to Ernestine and Larry for me."

"Thanks."

Her initial feeling on hanging up was relief that he didn't believe her, that he wouldn't be asking annoying questions of her or Jamie. This was quickly replaced by a feeling that she had been insulted, that her having boyfriends was so not possible that they both knew it was a joke. She wanted to call him back and tell him she did too did too have a boyfriend, at least one, but thought better of it. If the trip was a fiasco no reason for him to know. If the trip was a success, she'd make sure he knew.

Ralph and Carole both got off work early Friday, with plans to spend three nights in Quebec. He picked her up at her office. They were both a little nervous, almost blushing, uncertain, excited. They spoke little, and on the plane Carole read a romance novel, a vacation escape. Ralph brought with him the courtroom drama paperback he had bought while waiting for Carole on their first date. He had set it aside and found it while packing for the trip. Perfect.

The bed and breakfast was lovely, clean and quaint, inviting and charming. They stepped into their room, Ralph carrying his bag, the host carrying Carole's, setting it down, then quickly leaving, closing the door behind him. Their room was on the second floor up a tightly-turning staircase. A tree bursting with new leaves filled the space beyond the window, a green, natural privacy screen. In the room were two overstuffed chairs, a small round table, a massive old dresser of uncertain stain, and a double bed with four pillows and a lacy comforter.

"Well" said Ralph.

Carole looked at him, smiling warmly. "Well indeed."

They went to dinner, then walked and explored. A juggler was performing under a street lamp, throwing three apples in the air, taking a bite out of one or another every few tosses, all the while delivering a monologue about apples, apple pies, the art of juggling, and how proud his parents were that he was not wasting a college education in agricultural science. He was talented and hilarious, and his donation bowl, painted bright apple red, was filling rapidly.

Back in the room they kissed, then Carole said "Who goes first?"

"Ladies' choice."

"The lady chooses. You go first."

Ralph slept nude, summer and winter; he had since he was a teenager. He thought that might be too abrupt an introduction, so a few days earlier he had purchased a pair of pajamas. Very plain, very beige. In the bathroom he took them out of their package and put them on, then stepped back to see as much of himself as possible in the mirror. In the store, in the package, they looked fashionable, but now he thought he looked like a gawky kid. He felt something scratching his neck, and reached back to find a price tag still attached. No scissors in his toiletry bag, he took off the shirt and bit the string until it broke. It seemed to him that he had been in the bathroom a long time, so he quickly put the shirt back on, took one more swig and rinse from the minty mouthwash, and returned to the bedroom. Carole was reading her book in one of the chairs, light from a small brass table lamp. She was dressed as before except that she was barefoot, her legs tucked under her. He stood in the doorway, his toiletry bag in his hand, and turned around slowly. "Brand new, just for you."

"Why Ralph, I didn't know you had such a flair for fashion. No, that's not true, I remember a certain date."

"So you like the color."

"Is there a color? I missed it."

"Don't you need to change or something?"

Carole had also been on a bedclothes shopping trip the previous week. Not sure how cool the room would be, she bought a cute, no other word for it than cute, flannel nightshirt and a gown with negligee. The night was comfortable, so she chose the negligee and gown. When she returned to the room he was sitting up in bed. He was on the right side, the left turned down and waiting for her. The reverse of the sides she and Ken had used. She hesitated a moment, and Ralph said "Wrong side?"

"No, I like this a lot."

"Me too."

"Oh, why?" She asked with a sly smile, removing her negligee.

"Turn off the light, get in bed, and I'll tell you. I'll tell you lots of things."

Carole turned off the light and got in bed, sliding quickly over and into his arms. They kissed, then she said "Why?"

"Because I'm right-handed."

"How subtle. The romance makes me weep."

"And while I am telling all, I think I should tell you that I never wear anything to bed, year-round. These are the first pajamas I have owned since I was fourteen and already I am feeling claustrophobic."

"Why don't you take them off?"

They woke at the same time, their nude bodies pressed together. They showered and dressed quickly, enjoyed the breakfast they shared with a young French-speaking couple who knew enough English to convey that they were newlyweds. Carole and Ralph toasted them with fresh orange juice. They spent the morning wandering through shops and watching the street performers. A beautiful young woman, possibly a college student, played a cello, her fluttering music held on the music stand by wooden clothes pins.

After lunch they walked some more, enjoyed other street performers, browsed. Ralph bought a miniature painting of a bowl of apples, inspired by the performer from the night before. A perfect reminder of the visit. Carole bought for herself two scarves and an English-French dictionary. For Jamie she found the perfect sweater, bulky and warm, the wool a mixture of fall colors: reds, cinnamon, light plum. Then they returned to their room, where they heard voices and walked to the window. Below on a patio a man and woman, likely husband and wife, held an earnest conversation in French. It appeared that they were deciding which of several plants, currently in plastic containers, should go in which of several empty pots on the patio's perimeter. Ralph and Carole made love, took a nap, woke feeling wonderful.

Saturday night, late, they heard an incredible group, all in their early twenties, performing in a round plaza where several streets came together. A man played trumpet, trombone, and baritone. A woman played tenor sax, alto sax, and clarinet. A man played bongos, timbales, congas. They played for almost an hour, and the tips were constant and generous.

Sunday was cloudy and cooler, and they spent more time in the room, kissing, talking, napping. They explored and shopped some, had a small lunch and planned on dinner at a Chinese restaurant that their host highly recommended.

The spicy, wonderful basil chicken had called for copious quantities of hot tea and numerous sips of ice water. Ralph's very full bladder dragged him from sleep at three Monday morning. He had been dreaming that he was in the bathroom of his grade school, and when he awoke he was pleased to find the bed under him still dry, so realistic had been the dream. Coming back to bed he found Carole deep asleep, her back toward him. Both of them naked, he snuggled close, put his arm around her and kissed the back of her head. Like a crashing wave he was suddenly so deeply in love with her that he felt he could cry, or shout, which given the proximity of her ears to his mouth would not have been the gentlemanly thing to do. He contemplated waking her to propose, then thought the better of it. Let her sleep. But he wanted to marry her, wanted her to marry him. Wanted her to want to marry him. Holding her close he fell back to sleep.

When Ralph woke, he was as certain as he had been hours earlier. He was going to propose. Going to do it, say the words, pop the question. But when? While he was thinking about it, Carole got up, slipped on her flannel gown and went in the bathroom. After a few minutes she returned and asked if he needed in. When he said "no," she took the clothes she had put out and returned to the bathroom and turned on the shower.

Carole was happier than she had been in a long time. She actually thought that, standing in front of the mirror, brushing her hair after her shower. "Hey, there, face in the mirror. Haven't been this happy in quite a while, have you, Carole?" Jamie's question 'Ya gonna marry him?' hung on a hook in her mind. She took it off the hook, looked in the mirror, and said softly "Yes, if he asks me."

"Why don't you ask him?" the mirror asked annoyingly.

"What if he says no?"

"What if he doesn't ask because he's afraid you'll say no? You shot him down twice before," continued the argumentative mirror.

"What if you shut up?"

Then it was Ralph's turn in the bathroom to shave and

shower, get dressed. Carole, Carole, Carole was in his head. The morning slipped by, one more pamplemousse, packing, checking under the bed, checking out.

To the airport, to the plane, to their seats. Fasten seat belts, seats upright, tray tables stowed and fastened. Push back from the terminal, engines speeding up, taxi into position. Flaps set, engines roaring, the plane began to pick up speed on the runway. Ralph leaned toward Carole, his nose touching her hair, his lips near her ear, and whispered a question.

The End

www.ingramcontent.com/pod-product-compliance
Lightning Source LLC
LaVergne TN
LVHW050632100826
845148LV00011B/1845

* 9 7 8 0 9 7 4 2 1 6 1 6 4 *